Defekt

ALSO BY NINO CIPRI

Finna

DEFEKT

NINO CIPRI

A TOM DOHERTY ASSOCIATES BOOK

NEW YORK

DEFEKT

Copyright © 2021 by Nino Cipri

Cover art by Carl Wiens
Cover design by Christine Foltzer

Edited by Carl Engle-Laird

A Tordotcom Book
Published by Tom Doherty Associates
120 Broadway
New York, NY 10271

www.tor.com

Tor® is a registered trademark of Macmillan Publishing Group, LLC.

ISBN 978-1-250-78750-7 (ebook)
ISBN 978-1-250-78749-1 (trade paperback)

First Edition: April 2021

To anyone who has struggled to find their voice and speak out

Defekt

Welcome aboard!

We are so pleased that you have joined us on this journey.

As a Special Exempt Employee, you are on the forefront of an exciting new era at LitenVärld. We are living in an exciting time of big changes. We couldn't do this without you. We are grateful to you, and expect that the feeling is mutual.

At LitenVärld, there is a place for everyone, and we want to help you find your place—then make it good enough that you'll never want to leave. This handbook is both a map and a compass. It's meant to orient you and help you find your way. It contains all of the information and resources you'll ever need to succeed, but you are allowed to talk to your Resource Management representative in the unlikely event that you want anything else.

Table of Contents

- **The LitenVärld Universe™ and Your Place Within It:** How it all began, and how this is going to go.
- **Orienting Our Own Moral Compass:** We'd be lost without it!
- **Known and Unknown Risks:** Acting fast is always better than acting slow, but it's not without its risks. Luckily, our

employees are adept, adaptable, and quick to learn how to mitigate them.

- **Shortsight and Farsight:** Do we know where we'll be in five years? Thirty years? Do we know what we'll be facing tomorrow? Next month? Is there any point at all in thinking about future consequences? Or should we treat every moment like it's something to be conquered?

- **Expecting the Unexpected:** A boring chapter about personnel policy. No real surprises here. ;)

- **There Is No Escape . . . From Fun!** Are you ready to get this party started? Well, this party was going for a long time before you got here, and will continue long after you leave. Here's how to enjoy yourself in the time you have.

- **When "Don't Be Evil" Fails, Try "Don't Be Boring":** It's worked for us since 1958.

- **Changing the World, One Room at a Time!** How to build a revolution in thirty-two easy-to-follow steps. Complete with diagrams!

- **The Journey Never Ends:** It's not the destination that matters! Time and distance are illusions!

Chapter 1

The LitenVärld Universe™ and Your Place Within It

After everything, it's hard not to think in *lasts,* the same way other people—normal people, real people—might think of *firsts.* Derek saw his share of other people's firsts as a sales associate at LitenVärld: fiancés wandering through the store with a scanning gun, marking out items for their first home as newlyweds. Visibly pregnant customers picking out changing tables and toys for a first child.

LitenVärld had a whole section dedicated to firsts in its online catalog: the Milestone Collection, a soft-focus, dreamlike collage of normal firsts for normal lives. The catalog was empty of people yet full of life, strangely voyeuristic. It made Derek feel like an intruder, gazing at the well-furnished spaces whose occupants always seemed to be just in the other room, on the verge of returning and discovering Derek's unwelcome presence.

Derek's own quarters were furnished mostly from the damaged-and-returned pile at the store, and while he tried to re-create the feelings that the catalog portrayed—warmth, comfort, welcome, family, belonging, *home*—in the end, there was only so much he could do with a repurposed shipping container on the edge of the back parking lot.

Not that Derek wasn't thankful! It was wonderful that LitenVärld provided housing for him, as well as his uniform, off-duty clothes, and nutritious meals. Practicing gratitude was a healthy habit of self-care, and his employee guide emphasized the need for self-care. He exercised before and after every shift, jogging around the expansive parking lot and picking up litter as he went. He stretched and did thirty minutes of yoga before bed, following along with an old DVD that had formerly been a decoration in one of the showrooms. He practiced speaking in the mirror, practiced his smile, practiced keeping his shoulders relaxed and his hands in a neutral position.

But he would look through the Milestones that he was missing, the many events that seemed to define everyone's life but his, and feel heavy, as if he were casting a second shadow, thicker and darker than his normal one, that stretched out behind him and dragged down his steps.

So: Derek's lasts, since he couldn't quite remember his firsts. He ate his last plate of LitenVärld meatballs on a Tuesday in February, accompanied by a Greek salad and a small container of ginger ice cream with lingonberry jam. He ordered his last half-caf skim latte that afternoon, and it was likewise the last time the barista—who knew his order, but only deigned to make it correctly about a third of the time—gave him a full-caf, leaving Derek slightly ill and jittery during his last evening break in his last double shift. After eating his last box of frozen lasagna in his converted container apartment, he went for a walk in the frozen fields behind LitenVärld to watch the sun set. For the last time, he walked up to an invisible line that he didn't realize demarcated the property and, for the last time, he turned around without bothering to think about what lay beyond the line of stunted spruce trees, returning to his shipping container to get ready for his shift.

The store had been preparing for LitenVärld's new VIP membership program. Disappointing sales numbers over Christmas had led to corporate pulling the trigger on the program months early, rolling out the initiative with a grand opening in March at select stores, including theirs. There was a sneak preview in a week for select customers that were part of the LitenVärld Universe loyalty program. Derek and a couple of other employees had been pulling doubles to build the new VIP lounge, converting a series of rooms at the center of the store into a closed-off section filled with high-end luxury furnishings, according to secret specs sent from corporate.

Small amounts of stress were good for you; they made you grow. He went into the bathroom to brush his teeth and get ready. On the advice of Tricia, his manager, he practiced his facial expressions in the mirror, repeating phrases from the LitenVärld handbook to himself until they sounded instinctive and natural.

"Nobody likes a sales robot, Derek," she had said during one of their check-ins, scolding him for his stilted delivery. "Customers want a human touch in their time of need."

A human touch in their time of need. The phrase had felt so powerful that it had become a mantra for him.

"What can I help you with today?" Derek asked his reflection. Eyebrows raised and tilted slightly to signal a polite inquiry, hands loose near his hips, shoulders set back at an unthreatening angle. "What can I *help* you with today? What can I help *you* with today?"

That was when he noticed the tenderness, the croak in his

voice. He tried to clear his throat and winced in pain. Derek leaned toward the mirror and stretched his mouth open wide; nothing looked strange in the harsh, fluorescent light.

He'd heard Tricia complaining about workers getting sick—either coming to the store when they should have stayed home, or staying home when they were obviously faking being ill. He'd never felt the need. There was a phone number he could call if he experienced any physical issues; it was posted on the first page of his LitenVärld employee manual, the numbers large and stark. He felt an inexplicable sense of disquiet about calling it. It seemed like a waste of time to report just a sore throat. He pressed his fingers flat against his throat, prodding at the soreness.

He'd hold off on calling them. He didn't want to want Tricia to complain about him the way she complained about his coworkers.

. . .

Derek arrived at the empty store just as the last closing-shift workers were leaving the store. One or two nodded to Derek out of compulsory Midwestern politeness, and he smiled back (mouth closed, corners raised in a closed-off smile, respectful of their disinterest in conversation). The rest ignored him, which was normal. He wished there were an easy way to bridge the gulf between them, a team-building exercise or icebreaker that would unlock actual friendship with his teammates. But they seemed universally put off by Derek's friendly overtures, and it upset him that he didn't know what he was doing wrong. He'd asked Tricia, his manager, for advice, but she'd told him to keep his eyes on his own work.

Tricia was waiting just inside the front doors, tapping her foot impatiently.

"I don't suppose you saw Jules on your way in?" she asked.

"No, but I'm early," Derek said. He always arrived a minimum of ten minutes before his shift started. Sometimes earlier, if the boredom and silence in his container overwhelmed him.

Tricia huffed. "God damn it. Jules is on thin ice, I swear."

Derek wanted to think that speaking to him like this signaled that Tricia considered him a peer, capable of discretion. He didn't like to think that she knew nobody would bother to listen to him.

"Well, I'll be downstairs!" he said. "Have a good night, Tricia!"

She grunted at him, and Derek cut through the children's section, swung left past a cluster of open-concept living rooms and kitchens, and descended down the stairs to the cavernous basement, where they did all the assembly and stocking for the store. When Jules came down about fifteen minutes later, Derek had already made a dent in their assembly quota for the night. It was a relatively easy load-in/load-out: three showrooms, two of them under 150 square feet, including a children's playroom with no heavy furniture.

"Hey, Derek," Jules said.

Jules had been a seasonal temp who'd been upgraded to permanent, though they weren't a great fit, in Derek's opinion. He'd learned to spot the ones who would never belong—who, astoundingly, didn't *want* to belong. Jules remained as seasonal as a fad for blush tones or oxidized oak. They didn't have the staying power of an Arc lamp or Eames chair. At least they were friendly, more than Derek could say for some of his coworkers.

"Mind if I turn on some music?" they asked.

"Not at all," Derek replied cheerfully.

The daytime stocking team had a radio that switched between Mexican pop music, hip-hop, and classic rock, depending on the shift lead at the time. Jules didn't use the radio, but instead plugged in their phone to its auxiliary port. They put on something angry, soulful in a guttural way, which made Derek frown; punk was his least favorite musical genre. It was so alienating, purposely distasteful. Still, if he tuned out the lyrics and the underlying antipathy, the beat made a good rhythm to assemble the furniture to.

Or, it did for him. Jules seemed distracted, slow, and had a hard time navigating the instructions, flipping back and forth between pages in the manual. Their poor efficiency made Derek anxious. He had assembled three-quarters of a room by the time Jules put together a single child's toy chest. Derek could read the name SVINLÅDA across the empty box. The SVINLÅDA were a recent addition to the children's section, a small toy chest shaped like a pig. It was upholstered in soft pink faux leather, with a soft snout, ears, and a curly tail. The back was hinged, pulling up to reveal a space to store knick-knacks or toys. It was cute, but not overly complicated.

"Would you like some help?" Derek asked. It came out more strained than his normal tone. He could easily imagine Tricia's frown. *A human touch in their time of need, Derek.* This wasn't a scenario he had practiced for.

"I'm fine," Jules said sharply.

Derek nodded and went back to his modular shelving unit. Message received, loud and clear.

"Actually," Jules said a moment later, tossing down their hex wrench. "I'm not fine. Actually, everything is shit, I hate this job, I hate my life, and I really just want to get high and listen to *Purple Rain* on repeat while sleeping until May."

Derek twisted his hex wrench nervously between his fingers. "I'm sorry to hear that."

He cringed a little at how hollow and practiced it sounded. His throat twinged again, and he cleared his throat. "If you want to take a break, I can keep working."

"No, you don't have to—"

"It's fine, really," Derek said, trying to project reassurance, overly aware of how trite he sounded. "I can finish this room myself."

"I don't need a break, Derek," Jules said. "I need these stupid instructions to make sense, and for feelings not to exist, and I need Tricia not to fire me before my health insurance kicks in so I can get a new pair of glasses. And none of those are things you can help me with," Jules finished. "So let me be miserable in peace, alright?"

They continued working in silence, aside from the caterwauling and power chords. Derek's hands moved automatically; he didn't even have to look at the instructions, really. Putting together the flatpacks was intuitive for him.

"What if you unpacked, and I assembled?" Derek suggested gently. "I've always found breaking down cardboard to be very relaxing."

Jules sighed. "I hear I'm good at breaking things." They abandoned the SVINLÅDA and started stomping on cardboard. Derek, showing what he thought was a lot of restraint, did not tell them that there were more efficient ways to flatten the boxes.

Their work progressed much more smoothly after that. This was the part of his job that Derek loved the most. He was made for sales, he knew. He excelled at it. Working with customers was a rewarding challenge. But he felt most at ease when future pieces of someone's home were coming together beneath his hands. And whatever Jules had meant by their earlier comment, they were good at breaking down the boxes, stacking the cardboard that could be recycled by the cargo doors. Derek let himself fall into the pleasant rhythm of putting together pieces of someone's future home.

"What the *fuck*?!" Jules cried. Derek turned to see them scrabbling away from the flatpack they'd been breaking down, orange box cutter abandoned on the ground. A thick, opaque white fluid leaked from where they'd scored a line in the cardboard.

"Is everything okay?" Derek asked.

"I don't know, is it *okay* for a box to start oozing like that?" Jules said.

Sometimes LitenVärld shipped items in strange packaging, and they arrived in the store wrapped in dried kelp or boxes made of some brittle clay that smelled like baker's yeast or sulfur. One of corporate's "green" initiatives, Tricia had assured him.

She apparently hadn't given Jules the same heads-up.

"Yeah, they do that sometimes," Derek said. He wasn't sure what the big deal was. "You didn't get any on you, did you? Sometimes it can cause a rash."

Jules stared at him, and Derek felt a small flutter of panic. Had he said something weird? He'd just been trying to reassure Jules. Maybe this was why Tricia had told him not to try to make friends with his coworkers.

"There are work gloves, if you want," he tried. "You're supposed to bring your own, but I keep a pair stashed—"

"Are we really going to gloss over the fact that the box was leaking *sap*? Is that not creeping you out at all?"

Derek toyed nervously with his wrench. "What's so bad about that? It's eco-friendly. And if you wear gloves like the handbook suggests—"

"I should have known not to expect you to get it," Jules said sourly. "You're the creepiest thing in this stupid store."

In the echoing silence that ensued, Derek noted that Jules looked about as shocked as he felt. Did they feel it too? Like something had just reached down their throat and grabbed their guts with a tight, unrelenting grip?

"I'm— Shit, Derek, I'm so—"

"It's fine," he said. "Don't worry about it. I, I always appreciate feedback, and will—"

The odd ache in his throat suddenly cracked into sharp pain, like he'd just swallowed a mouthful of broken glass.

Jules looked over as Derek dropped his hex wrench, which hit the floor with a jangling crash. "Derek?" they asked. "You okay?"

"Ow," he said—or tried to say. Something had blocked his throat—not so he couldn't breathe, but too big to swallow around or speak comfortably through. He coughed into his elbow, and whatever was in his throat seemed to move, uncoiling in the hollow of his throat. His mouth flooded with the taste of salt and copper, and he felt vileness pass his lips.

"Derek?" Jules said urgently. "Are you choking? Do you need help?"

Derek cautiously lifted his mouth away from his sleeve. Something red, wet, and gristly had splattered against his uniform. He wiped his mouth and clapped a hand over his sleeve so Jules wouldn't see.

"Fine," he said, edging toward the bathroom in the back of the assembly room.

"Is that blood?" Jules asked.

"I just need . . ." He wasn't sure *what* he needed, so he fled without finishing his sentence.

• • •

The basement bathroom was for staff only, and starkly different from the customer restrooms. The customer restrooms were another venue to display LitenVärld's varied aesthetics, with each stall designed in a different style. The new VIP lounge would feature cutting-edge designer luxury toilets, with bidets, heated seats, air dryers, white noise machines, and self-raising and -closing lids. The premiere model was inspired by Arne Jacobsen's iconic Egg chair, and its wide back and arms offered pressure point massage meant to stimulate the digestive system. It was designed to sync to the user's phone to play music, but corporate had instructed that all the showroom versions play only Debussy.

The bathrooms in receiving and assembly were, by contrast, terrible. One toilet didn't have a seat cover. Another stall had lost its door. The third toilet was an unsettling shade of avocado green with a carpeted lid. Management had covered graffiti left by disgruntled employees in mismatched patches of brown paint, which dotted all the walls. The only source of light was a buzzing fluorescent bulb, which tinted everyone's skin a cold and sickly blue, and the mirror was scratched across its surface with the graffiti-ghosts of long-ago employees. Derek kept his gaze on his reflection as he pulled off his Liten-Värld polo shirt and stuck its sleeve under the faucet, running it under the too-hot water. Faint swirls of red curled in the basin as it filled with steaming water. Against his bluish, washed-out skin, the blood flecking his chin stood out, almost black.

His reflection looked strange, unfamiliar—like a word repeated over and over until it sounded like gibberish, his face suddenly looked like something he had never seen before. He stretched open his mouth, trying to angle his chin up to see down his throat, but he couldn't make out anything in the terrible light.

He should call the number in his employee manual. The instructions were very clear: *If you experience any signs of illness, injury, hallucinations, personality changes, phantom limb pain, sudden hemorrhaging, inexplicable subdermal growths, or other physiological abnormalities, call the following number immediately and await further instruction.*

Derek's hands clenched against the sodden fabric of his uniform polo, anxiety temporarily overriding the pain in his jaw and throat. He had to call the number. Something had gone wrong, and whoever was on the other end of the line would tell him how to make it right again. He did not want to call the number, though, somehow sure that the cure would be worse than what he was feeling.

There was a cautious knock at the door. "Derek?" Jules called through the wood. "Are you okay?"

Derek's throat was clenched too tight to answer. He spat into the sink, rinsed the thick, dark material that came out of him down the sink without examining it. If he didn't see it, he wouldn't have to report it.

"I'm fine!" he said. His voice was hoarse, but hopefully his tone was normal. All that practice in the mirror was coming in handy. "But would you mind getting me a fresh polo?"

There was a pause, then Jules said, "Alright. Medium?"

"Large, please."

He couldn't unclench his fingers until he heard their footsteps retreating from the door. Derek turned his eyes back down to the sink. Most of the shirt was sodden navy blue, but a red-brown stain stood out on the right sleeve, where he had covered his cough. "Dang it," he hissed.

Jules didn't bother knocking when they returned, and their reappearance badly startled Derek.

"I could only find a medium and an XXL, so I brought... Are you okay?" Jules said, staring at Derek. "You look really messed up."

"Must be the light," Derek said nervously. His throat felt like it was on fire, but he didn't dare try to cough again. "I'll take the medium."

Jules didn't stop staring at him. "You still have some... something on your jaw."

Derek pawed at his face.

"Other side. No, it's—alright, it's gone."

Caught red-handed, Derek thought to himself. He wiped the blood discreetly onto a paper towel.

"Shirt?" he asked. He always felt naked without his uniform, and the feeling was more acute with someone staring at him in his threadbare undershirt. Jules tossed him the sky-blue polo. Derek slipped it over his head, the fabric stiff and starchy against his over-sensitized skin.

"Sorry," he said. Jules seemed wary of him now, suspicious. He was used to being functionally invisible to his coworkers, and their scrutiny made him feel hotly embarrassed. "I didn't mean to worry you. I'm fine, really."

"Maybe you should go to urgent care or something?" Jules said. "You're on the company insurance, right? I know you got hired before me."

Derek opened his mouth, then closed it. Was he on Liten-Värld insurance? Tricia had never told him, and insurance wasn't discussed in his employee handbook at all.

"You should at least go home for the night," Jules insisted.

"I need to find an employee handbook," Derek said. "There's a phone number to call."

Jules looked at him sidelong, a single eyebrow perking up in disbelief. "If you don't have money for a co-pay, I can spot you—"

"Just help me find the book, please?" he pleaded.

Jules looked like they wanted to argue more, but put their hands up and shrugged. "Pretty sure there's one in the breakroom."

• • •

The breakroom was all the way in the back of the store, furnished with the same worn, patchwork, utilitarian style as the receiving and assembly area. There was a row of dented metal lockers painted an industrial gray, a table that wobbled on the warped linoleum floor, with mismatched chairs scattered around it. On the wall opposite the lockers, there was a bulletin board with Department of Labor–issued flyers in English, Spanish, and Arabic. A battered blue binder hung from some twine on a peg, the word HANDBOOK written sloppily across it in fading black marker.

Derek grabbed it, flipping to the page that he knew included the number to call.

Policies for new hires: the importance of maintaining boundaries against fraternization outside of work.

Derek stared blankly at the page, his brain refusing to parse the words. "There's supposed to be a phone number," he said, flipping back. "That you call if you feel unwell."

Jules pried the book out of his hands and flipped to the table of contents—which was definitely not the same as Derek's. It had dozens of chapters, all of which had much more plainspoken, descriptive titles than the ones he remembered: *Equal Opportunity Employment and Non-discrimination/Non-harassment Policies; Benefit Schedule for Non-Exempt Workers; Clearance Sales, Special Inventories, and Other Notable Changes in Normal Procedures.* Jules seemed to find what they were looking for toward the bottom, and paged through the book until they were nearly at the end. "Is this what you mean?" they asked, tapping the top of the page with their finger.

LitenVärld Wellness Helpline
Call for free professional medical advice!
Open 24/7/365!

"I guess?" Derek said. There was no mention of phantom limb pain or hallucinations. He must have a newer version of the handbook at home; this one looked old, a photocopy of a photocopy.

He fumbled his phone out and dialed the number. There was a pleasant five-tone jingle when the call went through.

"Välkommen! You have reached the twenty-four-hour Liten-Värld Family Wellness Helpline! Please enter the store number where you work."

Derek entered the six-digit number he'd memorized on his first day.

"Thank you! Our team of medical professionals are currently

getting their daily recommended seven-point-five hours of rest, but leave a message and a callback number, and we'll get back to you ASAP."

Derek stammered out his phone number, then added, "I've been having some symptoms. Uh. A cough and sore throat." He glanced at Jules. "Some other symptoms that I'd rather not talk about over the phone."

Jules's eyes widened a bit, and they took a step back as Derek left a callback number and finished the message.

"Thank you! We can see that you are calling from ..." There was a brief pause, then an entirely different voice intoned, *"COOK COUNTY, ILLINOIS."* The other voice popped back, calm and cheerful. *"Please be advised that all employees in COOK COUNTY, ILLINOIS, are granted a minimum of ONE HOUR OF PAID SICK LEAVE FOR EVERY FORTY HOURS WORKED, UP TO A MAXIMUM OF FORTY HOURS IN A SINGLE YEAR. If you feel under the weather, please let your manager know—they'll be able to calculate how much of your sick leave remains. We encourage everyone in the LitenVärld family to take their health seriously, and to utilize their sick leave in a responsible manner. To repeat this message, please press—"*

Derek hung up, and absently wiped away the sweat that had gathered on the back of his neck.

"We get sick leave?" Jules asked. They must have overheard the recording. "Since when? Nobody ever told me that."

"I don't know," Derek said. He couldn't recall the topic even being mentioned in his handbook.

"You should definitely take tomorrow off," Jules said.

"I'm fine to work," Derek said automatically. The anxiety in his chest pressed down, heavy and leaden. "I've never missed a shift before. I can't miss a shift."

"None of us can afford to catch whatever you've got. Seriously, call in tomorrow. I'll tell Tricia you were coughing up blood."

Derek tried to scoff. "That wasn't—I didn't—I've never missed a day before, and I'm not going to start—"

"Don't be a fucking tool, Derek!" Jules shouted. "Just take a day off!"

A blush was spreading across Derek's face, and shame squirmed in his chest.

Derek *hoped* that squirming was shame.

"I'll go home," he said.

"And call in sick tomorrow," Jules said. "I'm working tomorrow and I *will* snitch on your bloody cough if I see you."

"Fine!" Derek said. "I still think this is a huge overreac—"

He choked on the last word as something moved in his throat again, jumped up and squirmed against his soft palette. Derek gagged, clapped a hand over his mouth, and sprinted toward the closest bathroom—the VIP restroom. Derek ducked through three showrooms and hurdled over a kitchen table before slamming open the door and shouldering open one of the stalls.

The egg chair toilet stood before him, greeting him with strains of one of Debussy's *Études*. Its armrests stretched wide and welcoming, the beautiful curves of its bowl ready and waiting to receive him.

• • •

Derek's conversation with Tricia was . . . odd.

"I need to take a sick day," he told her, once he'd nervously run through his compulsive pleasantries. His hands had been shaking since he'd pushed himself away from the egg chair toilet, wiped red-tinged foam from his lips, and had to breathe through several minutes' conviction that his entire world was ending, accompanied by tinny electronic piano music.

"A what," she said flatly.

"A sick day," he repeated. "I did the calculations, and I should have saved up at least twelve hours according to Cook County law." It should have been more than that, but Derek decided to only calculate hours when he was officially on the schedule, not just clocked in for extra time or subbing in for a missing coworker.

There was an uncomfortably long pause. Derek's resolve buckled under the silence.

"I can still come in, if you—"

"*Derek!*" Jules hissed; they'd refused to go back to work until he called Tricia. They swiped their hand across their throat.

He cut himself off and waited to hear Tricia's answer.

"Did you call the number, Derek? In your handbook?"

"Yes. They told me about the sick leave and encouraged me to use it."

"I see," Tricia said doubtfully.

"I should be fine for my next shift," he said. "I'm sure it's just a, a passing thing. A twenty-four-hour bug." He was pretty sure he'd heard other workers say that. He'd never been sick a day in his life, so this was all new to him.

"Okay," Tricia said. "I . . . hope you feel better."

She said it with the same absence of conviction, like this was strange, unnavigable territory for the both of them.

"That's great, thanks so much, have a good night." The words slipped out automatically; it was one of the phrases he'd practiced in the mirror.

"Good," Jules said when he hung up. "Go home. And go to urgent care if anything else happens. You looked real bad there for a second."

Derek nodded wearily, too worn down to fight anymore.

Derek felt himself warm. He'd assumed that Jules was too much of a transient soul to ever really be part of the LitenVärld family. But maybe they weren't such a temporary worker after all.

He tried to convey some of this sentiment to Jules, but he felt a little loopy, dizzy, like when he stayed awake too late assembling and disassembling shelving units in his apartment to relax.

"I'm just trying to say that you're family," Derek said earnestly. "The LitenVärld family. That means a lot to me."

Jules smiled uncertainly. Maybe he'd been *too* earnest. He'd been cautioned against that; nobody liked a robot, but nobody liked Derek's occasional frightening, intimidating sincerity, either. Still, saying the words aloud soothed something in him, coolness spreading through the rawness in the back of his throat.

"Thank me when you're better," Jules said, the last time they ever spoke to Derek. "If that's what you're trying to do."

Derek stumbled back to the other side of the building, past the loading dock where they'd been working, down a small, narrow path to a series of shipping containers that stood in spreading rings of rust on the cracked pavement. There was a smaller one toward the back; that was where Derek lived. Not a home, per se, but home enough.

Derek crawled up into his loft bed and slept for close to thirty hours.

Our corporate values

1) Change is the only constant.

We are constantly looking not just ahead, but up and down, side to side, and around corners. You never know what new strangeness will be waiting for you on the other side of this moment.

Change is often uncomfortable, until it isn't anymore.

As a member of the LitenVärld family, your job might not always be pleasant, comfortable, or easy. By taking this job, you agree to step out of your comfort zone. We are not looking for acceptable people, or even good ones—we are looking for the extraordinary. Working for LitenVärld means working in an ever-changing flux. You already know if that is something that thrills you.

2) The worth of loyalty cannot be measured ... but it can be rewarded.

Once you are through your employee orientation, you will enter the exciting, intersecting worlds of LitenVärld. Those that thrive here find a culture that is diverse, welcoming, and completely unique. Many are surprised to learn that our retention rate for the first year of employment is low. Those that do stay, however, find themselves less and less likely to leave over time. Your standards will change; your view of the world, your expectations of reality, your desires and dreams and personality.

To succeed at LitenVärld, you must allow yourself to be shaped by LitenVärld.

Becoming a part of our family may not be easy, but it's a richly rewarding experience.

3) Innovation over everything.

Change is a constant, and we must always be willing to shift with it, but company innovation means learning to shape change to our benefit. We expect our employees to constantly strive for improvement—not just for themselves, but for LitenVärld and the larger world.

From *The LitenVärld Special Employee's Handbook*

Chapter 2

Orienting Our Own Moral Compass

Derek sometimes woke up to crushing loneliness, a shocking sense of isolation that made his chest feel as hollow as an empty cardboard box; as if all that held him together were thin slices of cheap packing tape and inertia. In the middle of that loneliness, he couldn't remember who he was or what his purpose was, why he was in a narrow bed in a small room, and most pressing, *why he was alone.* His solitude had mass, and shifted Derek's personal gravity toward it, pulling him down into a spiral of despair.

It wasn't every day; sometimes the loneliness was a little bit more distant, or he was numb to it, able to drown out the silence around him by thinking through the tasks that awaited him, grounding himself in what LitenVärld needed. He was necessary; he was part of the LitenVärld family, and he could not lie in bed stewing in his despair. His teammates and customers needed him!

Today, alone in his bed, he felt . . . okay. For once. He took a deep breath, and felt how it moved through his mouth and airway. Derek rubbed at his throat; it was still tender, a little swollen and stiff, but nothing like it had been. He found himself reluctant to move out of bed and start his routine. The languor pressing him down felt pleasant, like the ache in his muscles from a long shift assembling a new showroom.

Maybe this was why people got sick, Derek thought, then imagined Jules yelling at him that people didn't *choose* to get sick. Maybe this was why people took sick days, he corrected himself. Because somehow, it made them feel better.

He rolled out of bed and padded into the bathroom. After showering, he wiped the condensation from the mirror and stared at his reflection, apprehensive as he opened his mouth and tried to see into the cavern of his throat. Nothing moved in the darkness. He wondered if he'd imagined the whole thing, before his eyes caught sight of the sky-blue polo he'd been wearing during his shift, crumpled on the floor by the sink. He uncrumpled it; a wide, brown stain spread out over the shoulder where he'd coughed blood onto it.

Well, he hadn't imagined that, at least.

He looked back at his reflection. "Can I help you?" he muttered, then repeated it as he spread shaving foam across his cheeks and throat. "Can I *help* you?" Too aggressive, he decided, even if his voice was barely above a whisper. "What can I help you with today?" Better. "How can I help you today?"

He managed to almost finish shaving before it felt like his throat split open in pain. The razor jumped up over the swell of his Adam's apple. He dropped the razor in the sink, eyes widening as drops of blood hit the stainless steel basin next to it. He clapped a hand to his neck, smearing blood and white shaving cream.

Something under his skin moved.

Derek looked at his reflection. His throat felt tight, like whatever was inside him had circled around his neck and was strangling him.

"Repeat after me," his reflection said. It looked infinitely calmer than he felt. Blood seeped out between its fingers, but the reflection looked unconcerned.

What, Derek tried to say, but caught in the mirror's gaze, he couldn't open his mouth to speak.

"How can I help you today?" the reflection said, in Derek's normal voice. Derek's mouth moved, forming the words along with it. But it seemed like the reflection was speaking alone; beneath the warm blood and slick shaving foam, his fingers couldn't detect any vibration. And yet he could hear it.

"How can I *help* you today? How can I help *you* today? If you sign up for the LitenVärld VIP membership, you'll save twenty percent on this purchase and ten percent on all future purchases. Did you know that all purchases over a hundred and fifty dollars include free shipping? Do you want to sign up for our newsletter? Do you *want* to sign *up* for our *newsletter*? *Sign* up for *our* newsletter? If you spend fifty dollars today, we'll include a coupon for a free jar of lingonberry jam. A human touch. A human touch in your time of need—"

The cut on his throat yawned open beneath his fingers and gave a whistling shriek.

Derek threw up in his sink. He turned the faucet on, messily splashing water onto his face to get rid of the foam and the blood. He looked at the mirror again, relieved to see that his expression matched his emotions; generally terrified, utterly confused. The cut on his throat was a thin line across his Adam's apple, just at the top of where he'd been shaving. It seemed to have mostly closed up, with only a few dots of blood still welling from it. It was ugly, but it hadn't opened up. It couldn't have opened up.

Derek cleared his throat and said in a soft croak, "What can I help you with today?"

The voice was his, *really* his, not whatever stranger had been speaking from his reflection in the mirror.

A hallucination.

He left the razor in the sink, not looking at the traces of blood and shaving cream sliding toward the drain, and slapped a large bandage over the cut. After a moment's thought, he pulled on a turtleneck to wear under his polo. It was well within company dress standards, even if his sky-blue polo now clung uncomfortably tight against his torso.

• • •

Derek arrived only four minutes early for his shift, which felt nearly like being late. He pushed his coat into one of the square metal lockers and drank in the familiarity of the breakroom: the lingering scent of reheated lunches and burnt popcorn, the view out the windows of the wide, snow-covered fields beyond the parking lot. He tried to shake the twitchy anxiety that still clung to him and get ready for the day.

The opening shift meeting took place at the beating heart of the store: the customer service desk.

Derek felt himself calming down as he walked through the winding labyrinth of showrooms; he'd always found it meditative, especially when there weren't any customers, to walk past the empty rooms, which all seemed to stare back at him invitingly. They were small, controlled universes unto themselves, steady presences after an exceedingly strange series of events.

Derek's good mood abruptly derailed when he saw a showroom roped off with yellow CAUTION tape and PARDON OUR APPEARANCE! signs. Beyond the tape, the room was in total disarray. The chair was overturned, the modular shelving was leaning dangerously to one side with its contents strewn on the ground, and . . . was that dried blood on the ground?

"Zahra!" he hissed. His coworker had walked past it with barely a glance. "What happened?"

Zahra turned around to answer, but didn't look up from her phone. "There was a wormhole yesterday. Customer went through, came back all jacked up. And only one of the associates they sent after her came back too. Apparently the other one, you know, '*quit.*'" She took her eyes off her phone long enough to add air quotes to the last word.

That was how Derek found out Jules had disappeared into another universe.

Derek didn't have words to describe the feeling that left him with. Wormholes, or mashkhål as they were called in his handbook, were a rare but not unexpected phenomenon at LitenVärld. Their short entry, accompanied by oddly thrilling diagrams in the classic LitenVärld style, had ignited his imagination. He'd found himself longing for one to appear during particularly trying shifts, or when a coworker was rude, or when Tricia was harsher than normal in her feedback; the idea of being swallowed by another universe had its appeal, even while Derek knew he was too responsible to ever wander through a maskhål on purpose.

Losing the only coworker he'd felt a connection with to one, however . . . The feeling was an echo of the wild loneliness that blanketed most of his mornings, but compressed into a single, super-heavy point behind his sternum. He pressed his fist against the spot, but pressure didn't seem to alleviate it. It kept pulling his attention away from Tricia as she droned through the morning's announcements and updates.

"Derek."

His eyes snapped up from the floor. Tricia was staring at him. Everyone was staring at him. It startled him into a fight-or-flight response.

"How can I help you today?" he said, his grin feeling alien on his lips.

Someone snorted. Derek felt his smile wilt a little. His throat hurt.

"Let's talk before the doors open," Tricia said. "In my office."

The super-heavy point ballooned.

• • •

Derek visited Tricia's office regularly; there he received instructions and feedback, and occasional praise or rewards, like getting first pick among customer returns that couldn't be resold. He knew he had no reason to be nervous—he was an excellent employee, he strove always to embody Liten-Värld's values, and he had a 4.74 average rating on customer satisfaction surveys. But anxiety swamped him as he followed Tricia back to her office, made his palms slick and shoulders tense. Pressure was building in his throat again, and he kept swallowing compulsively, trying to repress the urge to cough.

"Did you enjoy your day off?" Tricia asked quietly. They were in the narrow hallway between her office and the breakroom.

"I—" Derek had to clear his throat. "I was sick. It was a sick day."

Tricia smiled at him, but her eyes held a cold, contemptuous pity. "Are you sure?" she said. Her voice dropped to an intimate whisper. "You can tell me if it was just—whatever kids call it these days. A mental health day. We all need to skip work sometimes."

"I don't," replied Derek, frankly a little insulted. "I wasn't feeling well."

Tricia stopped and turned to Derek, the force of her presence pressing him back into the dirty, scratched walls.

"Listen, Derek," she hissed. He was significantly taller than Tricia, but felt himself shrinking under her gaze. This close, he could see that Tricia had puffy bags under her eyes, inexpertly covered with the orange-ish foundation she wore, and her eyes were bloodshot behind the clumpy mascara. She would definitely benefit from her own mental health day.

"I'm listening," he said.

"I've already got corporate breathing down my back because of the VIP program launch and the maskhål. You being *sick* is the last thing my quarterly evaluation needs." She didn't add the air quotes, but she said "sick" the same way Zahra had said "quit," stretching meaning until it snapped.

"Is—is this about the sick leave policy?" asked Derek. "Because I checked and—"

"You're not sick. You've never been sick, and you never will be. You needed a personal day for—whatever people do. You spent the day soul-searching or reading poetry or jacking off—"

Derek sputtered, "That is *highly* inappropriate, and I don't—"

"Complain about it to the manager, then," she hissed, silencing him as effectively as a slap across the mouth.

Her gaze bored into him, waiting for a response. Derek didn't dare look away, didn't dare make a move. He had never felt so outwardly still, so inwardly chaotic.

Whatever Tricia was searching for, it seemed to satisfy her. "Are we clear? You needed a day for . . . call it personal improvement," she said. Her voice was softer now, gentle, soothing. "Repeat it," she said.

"Personal improvement," Derek said. He winced as he did; the words seemed to open fissures in the walls of his throat, but his voice sounded normal.

Tricia eased away from him, and Derek felt himself relax a little, the claustrophobia relenting as she put space between them. He tried to swallow, and pushed himself off the wall. "Is that all you wanted to talk about, Tricia?" he whispered hopefully. "Can I go back to the sales floor?"

Tricia huffed impatiently. "I'm not the one you're meeting with," she said. "Come on."

Tricia's entire demeanor changed when she opened the door to her office. The sharp, tense angles of her shoulders rounded, her head cocked at a friendly angle, and her smile went wide—wider than it ever did for customers or employees.

"Hey, Reagan!" she said, and the woman standing by Tricia's desk turned around. She was tall, white but with an even tan that seemed out of place in the Midwestern winter, wearing a well-tailored beige suit and heels. She was younger than Tricia, her hair a more natural shade of blond, her makeup a little more subtle. If Derek were asked to design a room for her, he would have put it in pastels and blush colors, overstuffed furniture, with throw pillows and blankets in nice neutral tones.

"Hey, Tricia," she said. Even her voice was soft—not in volume, but in texture. "Great to see you. I'm so sorry to drop in on you like this."

Tricia waved this off with a smile. "Totally understandable, given the circumstances. You know I'm always happy to—"

"This must be Derek!" Reagan said, cutting her off. She'd swiveled her entire attention to Derek, and he felt himself freezing. Reagan had wide-set, doe-like brown eyes, but Derek felt a thrill of anxiety shiver through him just the same. The room he'd begun building for her suddenly went a little colder. He pictured stark, abstract photographs appearing on the peach-colored walls, dizzying close-ups that were frightening in their immediacy—like turning around and finding something had snuck up on you.

Derek nodded. "That's me," he said, trying to smile without giving away how nervous he was.

Reagan regarded him for a moment before slanting her gaze impatiently back to Tricia.

"This is Reagan," Tricia said. The cheer in her voice had become brittle. "From corporate."

"I work in Resource Management," Reagan said. "I don't know if you remember me, but I oversaw your orientation at HQ before you transferred to Tricia's store."

Derek had no memory of meeting her, and that vague disquiet grew stronger at the word "orientation." "I'm afraid I don't," he said, unconsciously standing a little straighter. The spot behind his navel seemed to get heavier. His throat was suddenly burning. He was so thankful he'd put on a turtleneck before coming in.

Reagan shrugged, her smile growing wider. "That's fine," she said. "I'm happy to see that you've settled so well into your role here."

Derek let out a breath, relaxing minutely. His role here, yes. He could talk about that. "Oh, I love it here. I love my job. I'm so thankful to be here."

He only remembered afterward that his sincerity had a way of putting people off, making them suspicious. But Reagan beamed at him. "I'm so glad to hear that, Derek," she said. "Why don't you take a seat?"

Derek sat down in the metal chair, wincing when its legs screeched across the concrete floor. Reagan went around and sat behind Tricia's desk. Derek looked to see if Tricia would sit down next to him, but she seemed happy to stand by the wall, posture perfectly straight and attentive. Reagan ignored her, but Derek felt her presence behind him like a chill in the air.

"Tricia said that you called in sick yesterday," Reagan said, pulling out a manilla folder with a stack of papers in it. Derek wondered if it was his file: the only label on it was the letter *D* and a string of numbers.

"Just needed a—" He had to clear his throat. "A personal day."

Reagan nodded. "Guess you missed all the excitement from the maskhål then."

"Unfortunately," he replied.

"Why is that unfortunate?" Reagan asked.

"I . . ." Tricia's presence behind him seemed to grow colder. "I would have volunteered if I had been there, and I regret that due to my absence a member of the team had to go in my stead. Especially since one of them didn't come back."

Reagan glanced over his shoulder, back toward Tricia.

"Walked off the job," Tricia said coolly.

"And is that why you requested a new FINNA?" Reagan asked sharply. "One of your employees wandered off with it?"

Derek chanced a look behind him: Tricia's smile was stricken and slightly twisted now. She looked caught out, but quickly shifted into wounded. "It was lost in a collapsing maskhål while that worker heroically dragged an unconscious customer—"

"I read your report," Reagan said, dismissing her. She fixed her gaze back on Derek. "Anyway, Derek. You missed work and one of your coworkers disappeared. How does that make you feel?"

She clicked her pen and set the nib down onto the paper, preparing to take notes.

Lonely, Derek thought. Loneliness so sharp that it felt like his throat would split from swallowing it.

Reagan looked back up. "What was that?"

Derek hadn't spoken. Or at least, he hadn't meant to speak, and his mouth hadn't moved. "I didn't say anything."

Reagan shared another look with Tricia over Derek's shoulder.

"I'm not sure how it makes me feel," Derek said quickly. "Disappointed in myself, I guess. That I let everyone down."

Reagan smiled again, but it was smaller now, perfunctory. She looked behind Derek. "You can go back to the sales floor, Tricia," she said. "I'll let you know when we're done here."

Tricia's silence turned even frostier. Derek glanced at her quickly. She shot him an icy, venomous look before she turned to go, the thick heels of her Danskos clunking dully on the floor.

When Reagan turned to look at him, he felt the force of her attention like heat prickling on his skin. He could feel sweat starting to gather in his underarms.

"It's normal to feel disappointed when you let your family down, Derek," she said. "And we are a family, aren't we?"

"Of course," he replied. "LitenVärld is my family."

Reagan was watching him carefully. Derek fixed his smile on

his face, praying that it hadn't faltered. Reagan flipped a page over in her folder, glanced down at it, then folded her hands over the paper so he couldn't see what was written there. She leaned forward and said, "I'd like to ask you some questions, if that's alright?"

"Of course," he replied.

"Some of the questions might seem a little weird, but just know that there's no right answer here. We just want to know what kind of baseline you're operating on. Like a personality test!" she added. "Have you taken one of those before?"

Derek nodded, a little more confidently; he'd taken a personality test as part of a mandatory team-building exercise a few weeks before Black Friday. "It told me that I was the Disciple," he explained.

Reagan nodded and checked something off on her sheet of paper before folding her hands back over it. "Good," she said. "Let's dive in. And remember: no wrong answers. What we really want here is an honest appraisal of yourself."

The questions that followed were . . . odd. Difficult. The pain in Derek's throat turned sharper, grittier, as he confessed what kind of kitchen item he would be (a knife sharpener) and why (necessary, helps keep other tools at peak performance, able to take the sharpest cuts and still do his job), or come up with five uses for a pencil besides writing (doorstop, fire kindling, hairstyling tool, fidget toy, or use the graphite to silence a squeaky hinge). What did he believe that very few other people did? (That hard work, kindness, and understanding would always be rewarded eventually, though not often in the short-term.)

Some of the questions were genuinely upsetting.

"If you were on a life raft with a nun, an old man, and a baby, and you had to throw one person off to save everyone else, who would you choose?" Reagan asked.

"I . . . why do I have to choose? Why do I have to throw someone off the boat? Why can't we fix the underlying problem?"

"Answer the question," Reagan said.

"Wh-what background does each adult have? Do they have skills that—"

"There's no additional information," Reagan said. "You have to choose one person on the boat to drown."

"Can any of them swim?" he asked. "Why can't we draw straws?"

"Time's up, Derek," Reagan said. "Who are you throwing out the boat?"

Myself, Derek thought desperately, and this time he heard it; the word hung in the air between him and Reagan, softer than his normal voice and slightly muffled. He hadn't said it. He'd locked his jaw around the word the moment it came into his mind. Something had spoken it anyway.

Reagan looked up from the paper she'd been doodling on, bored with Derek's agonizing.

"Yourself?" she asked.

"Who would *you* throw overboard?" he asked, feeling hotly embarrassed and full of dread.

Reagan leaned back in Tricia's chair, tapping her manicured nails on the glass top of the desk. Her expression was cool and blank, impossible to read. Derek felt a flutter of panic beneath his solar plexus. What did she want him to say? He couldn't tell, and not knowing made him more nervous than anything else.

"I'm supposed to be asking the questions," she said. "But for the record: the baby."

Derek flinched. "What? Why?"

"A baby can't take care of itself. If everyone else died, so would the baby. Sentimentality isn't an attractive quality in upper management." She smiled brightly at him. "Besides, it's all hypothetical. Who cares if a nonexistent baby drowns? Who's going to mourn it? Its imaginary parents? The fictional nun and the old man?" She leaned forward. "You?"

Derek desperately wanted to be somewhere else. The sales floor. The receiving and assembly area. His shipping container. *Home,* he thought, and realized that he had no idea where or what that was.

"Of course—" *not,* he'd meant to say, but Derek choked on the last word, and had to hunch over against his coughing fit.

Reagan watched him with that same bright, impersonal smile. It was like watching winter sunlight reflect off a frozen lake. "Tricia mentioned that you were out sick yesterday," she said.

Once Derek's throat stopped spasming, he took a shaky breath. "No, it was just a, a personal day." He could barely choke the words out: "For personal improvement."

Reagan snorted. "That's not what you told the LitenVärld health line."

Derek flushed. He wasn't sure why he'd assumed that the information he'd said there wouldn't be shared with his managers.

Reagan was still giving him that cold, sharp smile. *Don't lie to me,* that smile said. *But don't tell me anything I don't want to hear.*

Derek swallowed past the ache in his throat. "I'm feeling much better. Very . . . improved."

"That's good," Reagan said soothingly. She flipped the

folder on the desk closed. "That's good. I'm glad."

"Is that everything?" Derek tried not to sound too hopeful. "Is there anything else I can help you with today?"

"I can see how you made sales associate of the month twice," Reagan said. Her smile had shifted back to what he'd seen first, a pastel quirk of her lips, no sign of the sharpness behind her face. "There's one other thing, since you mentioned it."

Derek had risen halfway out of his seat. He sank back down into it, biting back a frustrated sigh. "Yes?" he asked.

"Your appearance today is a little off," Reagan said. "Not up to your usual standards."

Derek looked down at himself. "I double-checked, everything I'm wearing is acceptable to—"

"Yes, but you're not an *acceptable* employee, are you, Derek? You're an *exceptional* one."

Derek, for the first time he could remember, did not feel a warm pulse of pleasure at being complimented on his performance. He felt scared—that's what that feeling was, that trembling pit opening up in his chest. Something had gone wrong. He had made a mistake somewhere along the line, and now he was being punished for it. He didn't know what the punishment would be, and he wouldn't know until it was being enacted.

He couldn't remember being afraid before. Not like this. He didn't like it.

"I thought this would be better than—"

"Than what?"

Reagan was looking at him very seriously. She didn't seem to blink. "I cut myself shaving this morning. It looked . . . unpleasant."

Reagan kept looking at him, and Derek hoped she couldn't somehow see through him; he thought of the razor clanking into the steel basin of the bathroom sink, and then the blood falling on top of it. The razor hadn't cut him, but he'd still bled.

"You know, I think taking a day off did you some good," Reagan said crisply. "How would you feel about taking another one?"

"I . . . what?"

"After the maskhål incident yesterday, corporate has decided to do an overnight special inventory at this store. We'll need a point person for the inventory team we're bringing in," Reagan said. "I think you're the best person for the job."

"I am?" Derek said. The change in her tone was jarring. "I mean, I'm always happy to take on an extra shift."

Reagan's smile tightened around the corners. "I'll go ahead and put you on for the overnight inventory shift. You can go ahead and collect your things and head back to your containment unit, take the day off."

"Should I tell Tricia?" he asked. He desperately wanted to get out of there, but he couldn't leave without at least offering.

"No need," Reagan said. "I'm sure she's lurking out in the hallway eavesdropping on us."

Derek stumbled up out of his chair. "Well, it was nice talking with you, Reagan. Please let me know if there's anything else you need."

Reagan watched him unwaveringly as he backed out of the office. He waved nervously to her before slipping out the door, closing it behind him. He took a second to sigh heavily in relief—cut short when someone cleared their throat behind him.

He flinched away, hands coming up to . . . what? Fight? Protect himself?

"Calm down, Derek," Tricia said, rolling her eyes. She was leaning against the wall a few feet away.

He thought Reagan had been joking about the eavesdropping.

"You're going home?" she asked.

Derek nodded, wiping his sweaty palms on his khakis, leaving dark, damp streaks on the fabric.

"Coming back for inventory tonight?"

Another nod. "What time should I be here?"

"Anytime after closing." Tricia sounded tired.

She edged past him into her office, kicking the door shut behind her with one heel. Derek considered lingering a moment longer, eavesdropping the same way she apparently had, then frowned at himself. Had one tense conversation with HR really made him into the kind of employee who would try to catch some gossip between upper and middle management? It had been a rough couple of days, but that wasn't any kind of excuse. Derek gathered his things from his locker and left.

Changes to normal operations: special inventories

It will occasionally be necessary to conduct a special inventory on your store's goods. These are not the same as the biannual inventory, which is an overtime shift undertaken by non-exempt hourly employees.

Your manager will be responsible for calling in the Special Inventory to corporate, but if you observe any of the following in your store, you should immediately communicate them to your supervisor. (For further definitions of these phenomena, consult the appendix.)

- Missing items that cannot be explained by theft or inventory mismanagement
- Unexplained blood, bile, or other bodily effluvia
- The sound of breathing
- The feeling of a persistent presence when you know you are alone
- Unidentifiable molds, fungi, or pests

If nothing is done and the problems persist, please use the special hotline listed at the end of this page, and your report will be heard. False reports will be investigated and may be punished by verbal warnings, written warnings, loss or reduction of seniority and other benefits, unpaid leave, suspension, or termination.

WE ASSERT ORDER IN A CHAOTIC UNIVERSE.
WE TAKE YOUR SAFETY SERIOUSLY.

From *The LitenVärld Special Employees Handbook*

Chapter 3

Known and Unknown Risks

Derek made his way across the parking lot, his toes aching with cold in his work boots. He'd never worked an inventory shift before, but his dread over the strange meetings with Tricia and Reagan had faded in the intervening hours. He was looking forward to being in the store after hours; he'd always liked being alone with the furniture, the rooms, the housewares. In the blue-black night, broken only by harsh yellow sodium lamps, the stalwart walls of LitenVärld looked like a fortress, all-powerful and endless.

Tricia was waiting for him outside the big sliding doors, silhouetted against the bright light that spilled out of the front entrance twenty-four hours a day.

"Good evening, Tricia, I hope your day was—"

"It was fine, Derek," she said. She handed him a cardboard box with the word INVENTERA printed on the side in LitenVärld's trademarked font, along with a handwritten note in permanent marker: RETURN TO HQ AT END OF INVENTORY SHIFT.

Derek peeked inside while Tricia fumbled through her ring of keys. The objects in the box looked like barcode scanners, though they weren't the cute, boxy gray ones they used at the registers. They were a dark, iridescent black with bright red accents. They were shaped almost like guns, and they gave off a dangerous air. Derek touched one gingerly; the material felt . . . almost organic? The color of the items shifted as he hefted the box, and Derek thought of oil slicks and beetle shells.

"So, I've never worked one of these shifts before, and I was just wondering—"

"The inventory team will explain it to you," Tricia said curtly. She yanked open the door and looked at him expectantly.

He hesitated, sensing that he'd done something wrong and wanting to fix it.

"Derek," Tricia said. "It's been a long couple of days, and all I want to do is go home, drink an entire bottle of pinot grigio, and fall asleep in the bathtub."

Derek felt compelled to point out, "That poses a danger of drowning."

Tricia's shoulders stiffened. "Get in the goddamn store, Derek."

Derek shuffled past her. Tricia tried to slam the door behind him, but the pneumatic hinge fought her the entire way, and it was an agonizing six seconds before she managed to lock the door. Derek, still confused and upset, gingerly waved at her through the glass. Tricia sneered, then turned away and stalked off to her car. A moment later, she peeled out of the parking lot, apparently quite intent on her date with a bottle of pinot grigio. Derek turned back to the darkened store.

"Hello?" he called out. Tricia had made it sound like the inventory team would already be here, but the store seemed very empty, Derek's voice echoing back to him.

Derek took a few steps into the store and called out again.

"Hello? I was told that the inventory team would meet me? Is anyone here?"

The front entrance opened up into a wide foyer, with registers to the left, obscured by shelves of clearance and sales items for impulse buys. To the right was the food court and Scandinavian market, a smattering of tables and chairs looking out onto the flat, ice-covered fields beyond the parking lot.

The main path through the store split into three a few dozen feet past the foyer; two made circuitous, overlapping routes through the showrooms, while the one on the right, which Derek took now, led more or less directly to the customer service desk. His coworkers had found his intuitive ability to orient himself in the store to be one more unbearable thing about him; most new employees needed a map and at least a month to make their way through the store.

The emergency lights in the store—because LitenVärld never went truly dark, a fact that filled Derek with an inchoate sense of pride and safety—limned the walls, with reddish blobs affixed at intervals and puddling on the floor. Glowing crimson strips lined the walkways that wound through the store, with arrows directing customers toward the exits.

Derek made his way to the customer service desk, thinking he'd be able to find the inventory team on the CCTV monitors. He dropped the box on the counter, but then stopped at an odd sound coming from some of the showrooms. The sound didn't make sense at first, an odd rustling like someone dragging a bundle of sticks along the floor. Derek stopped walking, trying to triangulate the sound's location. Had raccoons somehow gotten into the store?

Raccoons would be annoying, but he was on the clock, which made it his problem. He set the box of scanners on the customer service desk and listened again, ear cocked. The scraping came again, though with the layout of the store, it was hard to pinpoint exactly where it was coming from. One of the children's bedrooms, he thought. He ducked into a kitchen that dwarfed the one in Derek's container, then slid through a shortcut behind a set of wall-mounted shelving.

Few of the other employees knew as many shortcuts through the store as Derek did. It was all about efficiency; sometimes, to help a customer or a teammate, he needed to be able to traverse from Bathrooms to the Clearance section without having to detour through the Food Court.

Derek pulled the movable shelves back until he heard them click into place. The scraping came again, definitely closer now. Derek wished he'd brought a flashlight with him as he followed the sound. He paused outside a children's playroom. The scraping sound was coming from inside, so he peered gently around the corner.

Derek liked this playroom more than the others; it had a farmyard theme that was much more restrained than the princess- or superhero-themed rooms, and not quite as hectic as the jungle. The bed was shaped like a tractor, the walls were painted a calming sky blue, with wall decals of rolling hills, fluffy clouds, and tall sunflowers. There was a scattering of stuffed animals, including a life-sized plush of a donkey wearing a sunhat, and beanbag chairs that looked like hay bales. It was also the least popular kids' room; only farmers wanted their kids to grow up and run a farm, and farmer parents were kind of thin on the ground in the Chicago suburbs.

The scraping sound came again, and Derek's eyes caught movement behind one of the hay bales. Derek stepped into the room and the movement ceased, but he made his way cautiously over to the bean bags. Behind them was a big wicker basket, one of their larger models, about two feet in diameter. It stood upside down on the floor.

It didn't belong in this playroom, but a customer or another associate might have left it here by mistake. Derek wasn't sure how it could have made the scraping noise he'd heard, but he didn't want to worry about things he could only speculate on.

Derek bent down to pick it up, but something seemed to be holding it down.

He stared at the basket, annoyed that it had thwarted his innate compulsion to tidy, and that he could not think of any reason why it was stuck that made more sense than that: something was holding it tight and had no intention of letting go. Derek huffed angrily, got a good grip on the basket, and yanked it. A SVINLÅDA, which must have been stuck beneath the basket, teetered, nearly toppled over, then managed to stay standing.

This one must have been a different model than the one Jules had been assembling before; the ears on that SVIN-LÅDA had been small, neat flaps of faux leather that fell to each side of its vague face. This model's ears were nearly as large as a real pig's, made of a thin, leathery fabric, pointing intently forward as if listening for something.

"Huh," said Derek.

One of the ears flicked toward him.

Derek stumbled back, the sole of his shoe squeaking on the floor, and the SVINLÅDA's other ear twisted around to follow the noise.

"Okay," he said. "That's . . . No."

The last word slipped out when the SVINLÅDA gave an all-over twitch.

"No," Derek said again, like he was yelling at a customer's dog that had decided to relieve itself on the Astroturf in Backyard and Recreation. "No, don't—"

The SVINLÅDA took a step toward him, its stubby wooden trotter clicking on the floor. Derek backed up, trying to maintain space between him and the thing, but tripped over one of the beanbags. He hit his head against the fake tractor wheel attached to the bed, fell into the life-size donkey, and rolled onto the cold cement floor, clutching his head. When he blinked open his eyes, the SVINLÅDA seemed to be staring at him with its eyeless face, both ears upright in his direction. It took a couple steps forward, and Derek scooted backward, colliding with the smooth plastic side of the tractor bed.

"Don't come any closer," he barked at it.

The head tilted.

"Just stay where you are," he said.

The SVINLÅDA seemed to be listening to him. It gave an odd, snorting sigh and sat back on its haunches. The lid on its back creaked open and two long, thin stalks poked out, a darker pink than the rest of the upholstery. After a moment, Derek realized that there was an *eye* on the end of each wobbly stalk. One stared directly at him, while the other looked around nervously.

"Okay," Derek said. "That's . . . I'm just gonna—"

He started inching away from the creature, not taking his eyes off it. He scooted himself along the bed until he reached the wall, then groped along it until he could pull himself up onto unsteady legs. One of the eye stalks tracked his progress, the other still looking around nervously.

"You . . ." he started. "You're not going to hurt me, are you?"

The creature gazed at him expectantly, and something

about its posture made him unclench a little bit.

"You're almost cute," he said. "And definitely nicer than a raccoon."

The two tiny drawers on each side of the SVINLÅDA pushed open, and long, spindly, segmented arms poked out, with blunt, curving pincers on each end. It made the SVIN-LÅDA look a little like a crab. The two arms reached out toward Derek, and he twitched away from them, ready to flee. But they didn't seem to be threatening. The SVINLÅDA had turned its porcine not-quite-face up toward him, and the way the two arms stretched seemed... supplicating? Like it wanted something from him.

The eye stalks both zeroed in on his face. Then they drifted down, toward—

Derek held up the basket. "This? This is what you want."

The pincers clacked excitedly, reaching toward the basket.

As Derek hesitantly leaned forward to put the basket back in the SVINLÅDA's reach, a resounding crash from behind nearly made him trip. As Derek turned to look, he felt something snag on the basket; the SVINLÅDA had grabbed hold of one of the handles. It tugged again, not like it was trying to pull it from him, but like it was trying to pull Derek away from the doorway.

"What?" he asked. One of the SVINLÅDA's eye stalks and both of its ears were now trained on a point behind Derek and to his left, where the crash had come from. The other eye stalk's gaze bored into Derek, as it tried again to pull him away from the door. It was trying to communicate something to him, Derek thought, despite its obvious nervousness.

It wasn't afraid of him; it had been calm a second ago, even when *he* had been freaking out. Whatever had made that sound, though—that had scared it.

There was another crash, and that was the last straw for the SVINLÅDA. It tore the basket out of Derek's distracted grip and flipped it back over its squat, pink body. Then it started scooting away, the basket making that familiar scraping sound as it crept along the cement floor.

"Wait," he called, but slammed his mouth shut again at a terrifying groan, as if a steel beam were bending under terrible strain. It was accompanied by the unmistakable sound of rushing water, and Derek peeked around the corner in time to see an inch-deep flood wash over the floors.

Derek glanced over his shoulder, but caught only the rounded edge of the basket as the SVINLÅDA snuck under a curtain into an adjacent room.

Well. That hadn't been so bad. Maybe whatever had caused the flood and crashing sounds would be just as friendly. Derek squared his shoulders and reminded himself that he was a professional; if he could handle Black Friday, he could handle this.

Derek edged along the walkway between rooms, following the flow of water upstream to what was hopefully its source. The glowing red strips on the walkway wavered beneath the ripples of water as Derek made his careful way through the twisting hallways.

Derek flinched as he heard another groan wend through the air, stuttering out into a series of low, watery trills, almost too low to hear. It was impossible to see more than a dozen feet ahead of him. Dark rooms opened up around every twist of the walkway, their furnishings amounting to little more than vague, shadow-wrapped shapes in the dull red emergency lights.

Another pulse of water washed over Derek's feet, freezing

cold. Had one of the mains burst? The water rippled with each squelching step he took. Tiny wavelets bounced forward and backward as he walked. It seemed to be coming from the new VIP area, and Derek groaned a little. If they had to scrap the entire new VIP lounge because of water damage, Tricia would have a heart attack.

There was a crash, followed by another of those inhuman, inorganic groans. Derek froze, pressed up against the side of a refrigerator.

The water rippled again, lapping at the laces of Derek's boots. But he hadn't moved.

Derek looked up and nearly screamed when he saw the egg chair toilet squatting around the corner from him, white and shining, the dim emergency lights casting it in a forbidding crimson glow. Thick pipes trailed behind it, jagged and broken, still leaking water. The tinny sound of Debussy's "Clair de Lune" began, though the speakers must have been damaged; it was distorted and off-tune, the song lurching along like a confused dirge.

Derek forgot his fear for a moment, so confused by the sight of a $6,400 luxury toilet standing in the middle of the walkway. Who would move the behemoth toilet as a prank? He hadn't had to install the toilet, but he knew it weighed nearly two hundred pounds.

He put his hands on his hips, coming out from behind the refrigerator to look up and down the walkway. "Is this someone's idea of a joke?" he called out.

The wide back of the egg chair toilet rippled, and Derek fell silent, his mind trying to bargain with reality as he fought down panic. *Oh, the toilet isn't moving, it's just the pressure point massage system. It's not suddenly changing colors, it's just the re-*

flection of the lights on the surface of the water. It's not looking at you, it's just . . .

It was looking at him. Derek saw no eyes, no ears, no way of sensing him or his movements. But it knew he was there.

There was another ripple across the broad surface of the egg chair toilet. And then it just . . . faded from sight.

Derek's heart started banging against his ribs. Adrenaline sent prickles across his skin. It hadn't disappeared, it couldn't disappear—god, *could* it disappear?

There was a soft splash. Ripples. Derek tracked them backward, and saw them emanating out from a series of pinpoints in the water. Directly above them—a sort of blurred smear where the colors and light weren't quite right.

And the smear was creeping closer.

Derek turned and sprinted down the walkway, throwing up sheets of water with every stride. The water was difficult to move through, and Derek kept stumbling, slipping and nearly toppling into walls and appliances, barking his shins and hips on lounges and farmhouse tables. He could feel the egg chair toilet behind him, but he couldn't see it, not properly; just blurs of motion and arcs of water.

He managed to lose the toilet by tumbling over a TÖRN-ROSA sleeper sofa and wriggling through the gap on the other side of a showroom wall—the sleepers were a terrible hassle to maneuver through the narrow showroom doorways. Easier to cut through the wall of one room and shove it through the hole. Derek was trying to scramble up onto his feet when he heard the egg chair toilet collide with the wall separating them.

The modular wall was a couple inches thick, held in place by only a few bolts. It didn't stand a chance against the toilet. The wall pressed down across Derek's calves, pinning them under the crushing weight of the two-hundred-pound luxury toilet. He tried to yank his feet out, scrabbling against the smooth cement floor, but he was caught. He couldn't even turn over to face his doom. All he could see was his own reflection, wavering in the cold, metallic-smelling water.

He was going to die.

There was a high-pitched electronic whine, like a mosquito had melded with the shrieking grate of nails on a chalkboard. Derek assumed it was in his head until he felt a ripple of heat pass over him. There was a shattering sound, and Derek felt chips of porcelain hit his back and exposed arms. The egg chair toilet shrieked, and the weight on his legs vanished amid a series of retreating crashes.

"Found our liaison," a voice said from a few feet away. "And our first defekta."

The voice was strangely familiar.

A man stood a few feet away, feet planted in a wide, immovable stance, framed in a slanting pool of light. He wore dark coveralls tucked into shining black boots that looked like they were made for combat instead of inventory management. He was holding something in his right hand, aimed at the retreating egg chair toilet—one of the scanners from the box Tricia gave to him. He must have found them at the customer service desk.

The man stepped closer and crouched down next to him. "Hey, man. How are you feeling? Can you move?"

Derek knew that walk. Derek knew that voice, pitched low to calm an upset customer. He practiced it in the mirror but had never managed to make it sound this . . . this authoritative.

Derek stared into eyes the exact shape and color as his own, tried and failed to find his voice to answer.

The Derek above him shrugged and spoke into an earpiece. "The level four has retreated for now. But our liaison could probably use medical attention."

There was a crackle of static, and a nearly identical voice said through a speaker, "Great, I'm on my way."

Leadership lesson:
Are your outcomes CLEAN?

When setting goals for your team, remember that the outcomes you're shooting for should be CLEAN.

Circumscribed

Lofty

Economical

Assignable/Accountable

Not obviously illegal

Circumscribed: *Make sure that there are limits on your ambition! Our resources are, in fact, finite, and we need to make sure our priorities are taken care of.*

Bad: "We will stop wormholes from appearing in our stores and occasionally losing our customers and employees in them."

Better: "We will equip every store with the technology to find customers lost in wormholes and recover employees who didn't walk off the job."

Lofty: *While we want you to stay realistic, we don't want you to let go of ambition altogether!*

Bad: "Research and development will process new discovered technologies from other universes and report back on them to the Board of Directors quarterly.

Better: "Research and development will seek out disruptive new technologies from other universe that could revolutionize the retail industry, and report them to the Board of Directors quarterly."

Economical: *Remember our bottom line! How is your outcome going to contribute to it?*

Bad: *"We will improve employee morale and retention through appreciation programs."*

Better: *"We will improve employee morale and retention through appreciation programs, except in positions where high turnover will be more cost-effective in the long run."*

Assignable/Accountable: *Who's ultimately in charge of this outcome? Is it out of your hands? Make sure that someone is **accountable** for ensuring this outcome!*

Bad: *"Resource Management will roll out the new D-64598 program as soon as they can and will communicate with managers in participating stores about expectations."*

Better: *"Reagan in Resource Management will be the point person on rolling out the new D-64598 program in time for Q4. Managers at participating stores will be responsible for ensuring that their stores hit projected savings in labor costs."*

Not obviously illegal: *Use your best judgment here!*

Bad: *"We will create a pyramid scheme to get LitenVärld Universe members to sign up their friends and family to a monthly subscription lifestyle program."*

Better: *"We will create a multi-level marketing plan to increase LitenVärld Universe membership, by encouraging existing members to sign up friends and family to a monthly subscription lifestyle program."*

Postscript: *While we always want your outcomes to be CLEAN, remember that members of the LitenVärld family are never afraid to get their hands dirty!*

From *The LitenVärld Managers and*
Supervisors' Handbook

Chapter 4

Shortsight and Farsight

It was nothing like looking in the mirror. Considering his recent experiences, Derek felt grateful for that.

After scaring off the toilet, Derek #1 had maneuvered him to the Jamboree Playpen, where stressed parents could dump their children while they shopped, and two sales associates would ostensibly look over the kids and make sure nobody bled. It was set against the back corner of the store and somewhat closed off, with only one entrance. If Derek had been asked to name the most defensible spot in the building, this is where he would have picked.

"Listen to me," Derek #1 had told him, propping him up against a child-sized playhouse shaped like a suburban McMansion. "You're confused. You're hurt. You're probably wondering if you're hallucinating, or if you're really meeting a doppelgänger. As a result, you might be feeling uncontrollable rage—I know I did." He smiled reassuringly at Derek. "And still do, sometimes, but that's because our doppelgängers love to ride my last nerve."

Derek was not feeling rage; he was mostly feeling pain from his squashed legs and barked shins, his palms where he'd scraped them. He was definitely feeling a little awed by this new version of himself.

"I'm sure you have a million questions. And we're here to answer them. Just hold on to them for a little longer while we get you cleaned up and ready to work."

His smile seemed so warm and natural, like it had been carved by long years of good humor, like he had never practiced it a day in his life. Derek nodded, trying not to swoon.

Derek #2 arrived with a full med kit a couple minutes later, complaining loudly about the store's labyrinthine sales floor and getting their boots wet, then barking, "Holy shit, what happened?" after catching sight of Derek.

Derek looked between Derek #1 and #2, trying to figure out his place in this taxonomy. If they were Dereks #1 and #2, what did that make Derek? Shouldn't Derek get to be #1? Was he Derek prime? But Derek had never felt like a prime anything, he was always secondary to everyone's concerns, even his own.

"Do I have a concussion?" Derek asked.

Derek #2 knelt down next to him. "That's what I'm trying to figure out. Know what day it is?"

"Thursday," he answered.

"How did you get hurt?"

"I was attacked. By a . . ." Derek hesitated; not because he didn't remember, but because *a predatory luxury toilet that camouflaged itself* felt impossible to say.

Derek #2 smirked a little, continuing to examine Derek's head for cuts or contusions, moving down to his neck and noting the bandage curiously.

"Cut yourself?"

"Shaving," Derek said. "This morning."

Derek #2 rolled the turtleneck back up. "Do you know where you are?"

"At work."

#2 clicked a penlight on and shone it into his eyes. "And why?"

"I'm here for a special inventory shift." He blinked until the after-image of the light faded from his vision, and he focused again on #2. "So, are you me? Is he? I'm really confused."

Derek #2 sat back, and Derek tried to quickly catalog the differences between the two of them: #2 had longer wavy hair, pulled back in a tight braid that somehow softened the Derek's features. Instead of the standard coveralls Derek #1 wore, this Derek's uniform had cut-off sleeves and a collar dotted with an eclectic array of pins and patches: a skull, a raccoon wearing sunglasses and flipping the bird, one that said THEY/THEM BITCH, another that said THEM FATALE. Looking closer, Derek saw that the fabric of the coveralls was covered in a chaotic arrangement of drawings, patterns, and phrases. They didn't seem to follow a single pattern or aesthetic; Derek could make out animals, plants, phrases, and a random assortment of objects. The largest and most impressive were jagged, stark letters drawn above their collarbones, edged with a silvery paint to make them stand out.

D E F E C T I V E, they spelled. The C dropped down into the center of their chest like a fishhook.

Derek looked back up and saw that Derek #2 was watching him. "You . . . don't look as much like me, I guess."

They smiled. "I'm choosing to take that as a compliment. You can call me Darkness," they said, tapping a finger against their breast pocket. There was a name badge sewn on there, but whatever had been printed on it had been scribbled out, with "Darkness" handwritten to the side. There were a few other scribbles, making Derek wonder if they'd tried out other names before deciding on this one. Darkness jerked their head at Derek #1, who was standing vigil at the entrance to the playpen, scanner gun at the ready, checking each hallway at regular intervals. "That's Dirk. He takes his job very seriously."

That had never seemed like a bad thing to Derek. "There's nothing wrong with that."

Darkness's smile turned wry. "Yeah, that sounds familiar."

It was so weird, watching features that Derek was intimately familiar with form unfamiliar and unexpected expressions. It made him feel a little lightheaded. Darkness had moved down to Derek's legs, peering through the torn-open knees to examine the skin beneath. They hissed softly at what they saw, but Derek barely felt anything.

"I'm hallucinating," Derek said. "Right? This is . . . I can't possibly be—"

"Getting your pants cut off by your sexy double?" Darkness asked as they slipped a pair of blunt emergency scissors along the seam of Derek's chinos. "I know, it's just like a dream."

When the pant leg came away, it revealed a gash along the side of Derek's shin sluggishly leaking blood and dark shadows of bruises blooming along his knees.

"Or maybe a nightmare," Darkness said. "Yikes. Can you wiggle your toes for me?"

They went through his joints, Darkness running their hands over the worst of the bruises, pressing apologetically into them to see if there were any fractures or breaks. Derek felt too aware of the warmth of Darkness's hands, even through the nitrile. It made something flutter in his chest, alien and fragile. He realized, with a jolt of embarrassment, that he couldn't remember the last time someone had touched him on purpose.

"What's his status?" Dirk called back over his shoulder.

"Banged up but not likely to bite it," Darkness said, patting the last bit of gauze tape into place.

"We should get back to the others, then. We need to strategize if the defekta have already mutated this far."

"Defekta?" Derek asked.

Darkness maneuvered their body underneath his shoulder and levered him up. They smelled good, Derek thought deliriously. "The mutant furniture that tried to kill you. You don't think that monster toilet came out of the box like that, do you?"

Derek, who had gotten fairly intimate with the egg chair toilet *before* it tried to maul him, shook his head. "Wait, are you my *inventory* team?" he asked.

. . .

The only thing weirder than encountering your doppelgänger was encountering four of them. There was Dirk, who was like Derek if someone had used a planer on his edges instead of sandpaper, possessed of chiseled features and an air of resolute authority. Darkness was Derek turned inside out, all the alienation he kept firmly tamped down and contained within himself pulled out and plastered across their skin.

Darkness had helped Derek hobble over to the breakroom, where the rest of the inventory team had holed up, waiting for him. "Most of the employee areas are furnished in earlier-gen stuff," they had explained. "It's all safe."

And now there were two *more* Dereks: tall Derek and small Derek, though he could think of other binary pairs of adjectives to describe them. Early-thirties Derek and teenage Derek. Woman Derek and terrible cologne–wearing boy Derek. Curvy Derek and wiry Derek. Serene Derek and twitchy Derek, thrumming with energy. Derek with smooth, well-moisturized skin, and Derek with ashy patches over his elbows and acne scars pitted into his cheeks.

"I'm Delilah," said the tall, serene, older Derek with the good skincare regimen. She waved a hand at the younger, fidgety Derek next to her, who didn't even come up to her shoulder. "That's Dex."

Dex's eyebrows drew together, unimpressed as he cast a gaze at Derek's bruised, limping form. He *tsked* and said, "This bodes *real* well for the rest of the night."

"Remember our conversation?" Delilah hissed at him. "About not being rude to people you are meeting for the first time?"

Dex snorted angrily. "I'm just *saying* that we've been here for all of *ten minutes,* and the new guy already—"

"He's not new, he works here—"

Dirk cleared his throat pointedly. Dex and Delilah looked at him warily, but let the argument subside.

"Sorry," Delilah said, half to Dirk, half to Derek. Dex grunted, though it wasn't clear if it was supposed to be apologetic. Dex skulked over to the counter and jumped up on it, heedless of the permanently sticky patina of spilled coffee.

"It's fine," Derek said, watching in confusion as Dex took a picture of the dirty mugs that had been left in the sink.

"You probably have some questions," said Delilah.

Questions? Derek was so confused that he could barely articulate a coherent thought.

"Why are you all . . . me?" he settled on.

Darkness and Delilah shared a look. "Maybe we should start with something easier," said Delilah.

Dex was typing something rapidly into his phone. "Give it

to him straight, guys. He's gonna flip his shit no matter what."

Delilah whirled around and spat, "I told you to quit being—"

"Fine!" Dex shouted, jumping off the counter. "I'll just go do something useful, protect our asses from bloodthirsty deck chairs or whatever!"

"Dex, sit down!" Dirk shouted. "All of you shut up!"

Everyone froze, including Derek. He had never imagined his own voice sounding so commanding. It was alluring, but a little disturbing as well.

Dirk turned to Derek, his gaze momentarily cold enough for Derek to want to flee. It shifted back into something stern but still kind, and Derek felt himself relax.

"You have questions, and that's very reasonable. But we also don't have a lot of time. We have a job to do. Dex!"

Behind him, Dex flinched. He seemed sort of high-strung.

Dirk said, looking over his shoulder, "You and I can go start setting up. Darkness, Delilah, can you get Derek oriented?"

Delilah and Darkness shared a look, then nodded. "Sure," Delilah said.

"Great," Dirk said, unholstering his scanner gun. He stood in front of Derek, who found that he couldn't look away from his commanding presence. "What about you? Ready to hit the ground running?"

Derek nodded enthusiastically. "Yes."

It took an effort not to add "sir"—Dirk's air of authority seemed to demand it. But Dirk just nodded at Derek, then looked at the others. "We'll set up a perimeter and finish unpacking the equipment. Holler if you need anything."

He headed out of the room without a backward glance, walking with a confidence that Derek envied. Out of the corner of his eye, he saw a loaded glance pass among the other three. Delilah tapped her ear twice while holding Dex's gaze. He rolled his eyes, but nodded, following Dirk out of the room.

After a second, Delilah sighed and sat down at the table across from Derek. Darkness started moving around the dingy breakroom, examining the open bag of Veggie Straws that had lived on the counter since Christmas, the mugs the closing team had left in the sink *again*. Derek made a mental to note to wash them before he left.

"I really wish they gave us a handout," Delilah muttered. "A visual aid at the bare minimum. Grab those mugs, would you?"

Darkness grabbed three mugs out of the sink. They were all, naturally, LitenVärld VAKEN mugs, ones that had been chipped or cracked in transport, or returned by customers. They were all different models from different years, with slight variations in the design.

Darkness dumped them on the table between them. Derek wrinkled his nose, noting the thick rings of coffee stains. Darkness had a similarly dubious look on her face.

"Visual aids," Delilah explained cheerfully. "Where do these mugs come from, Derek?"

"Kitchenwares," Derek answered.

"Right, and before that?" Before Derek could give the obvious answer—receiving and assembly, of course—she added, "Before they come to the store."

" . . . Distribution?" Derek answered. Honestly, anything that happened outside of the store's immediate operations wasn't really in his wheelhouse.

"And before that? Where do they originate?"

Derek, after a moment's hesitation, turned over one of the

mugs and looked at the faded lettering on the bottom. "China," he said, though he wasn't at all confident that was correct.

"That one did, yeah," Delilah said encouragingly. "But those kinds of international logistics are complicated and expensive, right?"

"I guess," Derek said.

"So if you're a company that values change, innovation—"

"And loyalty," Derek added, happy to provide LitenVärld's third corporate value.

"Which is a nice way of saying control," Darkness said, and Derek frowned.

Delilah shot them a look, then picked up the explanation again. "So you're a company that deeply believes in all of those things, and also you have access to infinite other worlds and their technology. Why keep paying manufacturers on the other side of the world when you can technically keep everything in house? Control the whole chain?"

"The research and development teams are like nerdy magpies," said Darkness. "They pick up all kinds of weird shit, poke at it until they figure out how to turn a profit—"

"And that's how you get this," Delilah said, turning over one of the newer mugs and setting it next to the one Derek had flipped over. Instead of a stamp saying *Made in China,* there was an odd emblem. It looked vaguely like the Liten-Värld logo; a circle carved up by meridians into small, square pieces, but with a series of black dots arranged into a pattern within each square. There was a definite logic to the arrangement, Derek could see that immediately. He brushed his thumb across the raised dots, as if he could read it through the texture.

"It . . . it looks like a—"

"Barcode," Delilah said. She brought up one of the scanner guns in her hand and aimed it at the emblem. A bright red cross appeared in the center of the circle. Derek flinched as it whined, the same eye-watering buzz from when Dirk shot the looming egg chair toilet.

No blast this time, only a cheerful beep. Delilah put the mug down and showed Derek the display on the top of the gun.

- HKV811-0364-00
- NAV: 0332
- GEN: 6.3.3
- STATUS: **DISCONTINUED**

Delilah tapped her finger on the display as she explained. "Housewares, Kitchen, VAKEN, model number and color designation. This is a sixth generation, version 3.3, which was discontinued so we can't sell it."

"And 'NAV'?"

"NAVs are pocket universes where these things are produced en masse and stored for shipping," Delilah said. "LitenVärld found them lot more cost-effective than manufacturing and shipping in from overseas."

Darkness added, "Plus, they get to advertise as being carbon neutral and ethically produced, and barely lie about it."

Darkness and Delilah were warily watching his reaction. Derek wasn't sure why. "That's . . . amazing," he said. "I mean, seriously, it's amazing how LitenVärld has used the tools it has to make its whole supply chain so much simpler. And more ethical!"

Derek found himself grinning. He hadn't needed more reasons to love working for LitenVärld—okay, maybe until the past couple days. It was a huge relief to have one handed to him like this.

"Pocket universes," he murmured to himself. "That is such innovative problem-solving."

"I mean," Delilah began. "The method improved their bottom line, but it has problems of its own. There's a self-replicating mutagenic defect in some of the NAVs, and it turns LitenVärld's products into animate, murderous, mutant furniture. Corporate calls them defectives, or defekta in Swedish."

Derek's gaze was drawn, seemingly against his will, to Darkness's chest, and the word inked across the chest of their coveralls.

"Takes a defective to find a defective," they said coolly.

Delilah elbowed them in the ribs. "You're not defective."

Darkness leaned back in their chair. "I like it better than *discordant*." To Derek, they added, "That's what it says on all our paperwork. After LitenVärld learned all they could about what went wrong with us, they stuck us together onto a special inventory team to deal with their little infestations."

Derek spoke up, "Okay, but what *us*? Are you versions of me from another universe, or—"

"Whoa, sweetie, nobody is a *version* of you," Darkness said sharply. "Unstick yourself from the center of the universe."

Derek nodded. "Sorry, of course." They hadn't covered etiquette for meeting one's alternate selves in the employee handbook, which seemed like a bit of an oversight, frankly. It was so rude to assume that other people were spinoffs of him.

Delilah looked over at Darkness. "I think we've moved beyond mugs. Do you mind being a visual aid?"

"You want me to show off some skin?" Darkness grinned. "Always."

They stood up from the table, unzipped their coveralls, and slid them down their shoulders, turning to face away. Underneath, they were wearing some kind of tight athletic shirt with wide mesh patches for breathability. They pulled that up, exposing their lower back and shoulder blades. There was a fist-sized tattoo in the center of Darkness's back, which looked remarkably like the barcode on the bottom of the mug. Not an exact copy—Derek could see that the pattern of dots was slightly different.

The whine of the scanner startled Derek, and he saw another glowing red cross appear—this time in the middle of Darkness's back. "Wait!" he said, reaching for Delilah, then drawing back when she squeezed the trigger.

But there was just another beep.

"It's okay!" Delilah said. "It's only weaponized against the defekta."

"Yeah, corporate wouldn't trust us with real weapons," Darkness said, pulling their shirt back down.

Delilah flipped the screen around so Derek could read the display.

- HRD-64598-03
- NAV: 1874
- GEN: 3.7.9
- STATUS: **DISCORDANT**
- SP-EX-EM
- DIV: INVENTERA

"Human resource, model number D64598, from NAV 1874," Darkness recited as they pulled up their coveralls. "Third generation, number seven out of a production run of nine. *Discordant*"—they shot a look at Delilah—"but a special exempt employee. At your service." They sketched an ironic little curtsey.

Derek felt like his brain had gone offline. There was a connection he needed to make, that he should have been able to make, but it was like he'd received faulty assembly parts; two tab As with no slot B.

"I'm second gen," Delilah said. "So is Dex, but something happened during his nutritive growth stage, and he wound up five inches shorter and about twelve years younger than the rest of us. And I'm . . ."

She waved at her long hair and face.

"They call us discordant phenotypes." She elbowed Darkness again and said pointedly, "Not *defective*. Just . . . unexpectedly different."

Darkness threw up their hands. "*Discordant phenotype* wouldn't fit on my chest. I wish I could have seen the faces on those R&D twerps when you told them."

"Yeah, they weren't expecting me." Delilah smiled thinly. "I think the only reason they didn't discontinue me immediately is because they were hoping to figure out how it happened."

"And they knew Dex would take them all out if they tried."

"Yeah, it's not like he'll bother to listen to anyone else—"

Their banter passed through Derek unnoticed; *slot B, slot B, where is slot B.*

Delilah added, in a gentle voice, "If I had to guess, you're probably seventh gen. You were onboarded for the Christmas season, right?"

Derek stared at Delilah, then at Darkness, waiting for one of them to crack a smile and laugh. His teammates always laughed at how gullible Derek was, how naïve, and he'd laugh along with them. And his feelings would be a little hurt, and he'd feel a little bewildered—why didn't he know all the same things that his coworkers did? But when they laughed, at least the world would be right again, unchanged and understood.

But Delilah and Derek were both watching him cautiously, carefully—not waiting to see how long they could string him along, but checking to see if he believed them, if he was upset by what they'd said.

Derek stood up and walked over to the window overlooking the field behind the store and the highway beyond it. He pulled his polo and turtleneck up over his back, then twisted around to look at himself in the dim reflection. He breathed through the sudden wave of nausea as he caught sight of the same barcode in the center of his back, positioned where it was unlikely he'd ever see it without knowing to look.

"You okay, Derek?" Delilah asked.

Derek pulled his shirts back down and smoothed them into place. "I'm okay."

He pressed his hands to his mouth, breathing slowly through them until the shock wore off. Beneath the nausea, he also felt . . . satisfied. Like an open loop had finally closed, and some, at least, of his questions had been answered. Why was he here? Why did it feel so difficult to connect to anyone? Why didn't anyone else seem to feel this way, share his nauseating sense of alienation? Why was he always so alone?

"You're not alone," Darkness said, and Derek realized that he must have stammered out some or all of that. "Like, if nothing else? You know definitively that you're not alone."

• • •

Derek immediately felt better, more grounded, once he was wearing a pair of pants that hadn't been cut into strips.

Delilah had offered up her extra set of coveralls; Dex's obviously wouldn't fit, Darkness had cut all the sleeves off theirs and personalized them with buttons and doodles in permanent marker, and Dirk didn't say anything, simply looked at Delilah until she offered.

"This is . . . kinda nice," he said, zipping the coveralls up. He'd kept the turtleneck on underneath, though he'd ditched the too-tight polo shirt. Delilah had gone to find Dirk and Dex, help them with preparations for the rest of the shift, but Darkness had lingered behind. "I feel like I'm actually part of a team for once."

"You are," Darkness said. They were sprawled at the table, long legs kicked out, working on a half-done crossword that someone had left behind. "At least for tonight."

Derek nodded and echoed, "At least for tonight."

He peered over their shoulder at the puzzle, to see if there were any answers he knew or could help with. Darkness, however, seemed to just be filling all the empty squares with nonsense. As he watched, they carefully scrawled the word BUTTRUMPET as an answer for the ten-letter capital of Nevada. He snorted, then turned it into a cough when Darkness gave him a look of transparently fake innocence.

"Those mugs aren't going to wash themselves," he said. He stepped over to the sink and started running the water hot. He felt a little bit more grounded when he was able to do something with his hands.

"I don't know how I'm going to just go back to my normal duties after—" He made a wide, encompassing gesture, sponge in one hand and HJÄLPSAM soap in the other.

"Do you want to go back?" Darkness asked, looking back down at the crossword.

"Can I join you all instead?" he asked, sort of embarrassed at how the question sprang from him.

They didn't answer for a moment, but instead got up and stood next to him, picking up a dish towel and drying the wet mugs. "Careful what you wish for, Derek."

"What do you—"

"It's not that bad, you know," they said quietly, cutting him off. "Now that you know exactly what you are and what you were designed for, you get to choose."

"Choose what?"

"What parts of yourself to keep, and what to throw out and make up for yourself."

Derek's eyes drifted to the handwritten *DARKNESS* on their breast pocket, then the black and silver lines across their chest: *DEFECTIVE*. They were so close, their hip practically touching his. Derek didn't let people get this physically close to him, instinctively maintaining a proper one and a half feet between himself and his coworkers, two feet between himself and a customer. He'd never really questioned why he did it, while he looked at the way other people casually touched each other with a longing like a fishhook in his heart.

Maybe it was because they were the same person, that Darkness could slip through that invisible barrier that Derek maintained against the rest of the world.

"Is that what you did?" he asked. He handed them one of the mugs, now clean but still permanently stained with years of coffee. "You just decided that you were discordant and said,

'To heck with it, I'm going change my name and draw all over my uniform?'"

Darkness laughed sharply. "None of us *decided* to be anything. Delilah didn't decide she was a woman any more than Dex decided to have a critical failure during a growth stage. Del *is* female, and Dex is stuck going through puberty, and I am—how did Reagan put it on my performance review—a stubbornly independent thinker with an odd creative streak."

Darkness's impression of Reagan's chillingly smooth tone was spot on. Derek shuddered a little.

"All that gets labeled discordant. Can't carry the tune they want me to sing, so I'm making up a new one." They grinned crookedly. "It's a shitty song, anyway."

Derek asked, honestly confused. "I like the—the song, though. I like what I do, I like working for LitenVärld. I'm good at it. And I like what they've given me. It means a lot."

Darkness sighed a little. "It means what they told you it means."

They took the last mug out of Derek's hand, dried it, and then tucked it into a cabinet before going back to their crossword. Derek felt absence rushing in to fill the space Darkness had occupied, heavy as the loneliness that pressed down on his mornings.

"Dirk's gonna like you," they said. "He's a big company man."

"I don't know why you say that like it's a bad thing," Dirk said. He occupied the hallway between the breakroom and office, leaning against the wall. Derek had a brief flashback to that morning, Tricia eavesdropping in the hallway. "We're all company men."

"We are definitely not all men," Dex said as he walked past to the sales floor.

Dirk shrugged. "Fine. Two company men, one company woman, and one fluidly gendered company individual, who, despite all being genetically identical, can't even agree on the pizza toppings."

"Hawaiian or get the fuck out," Dex called back.

"Meat-za or bust, bitch!" said Darkness.

"Why would you get pizza when you can have a calzone?" Delilah argued from the hallway. "They're objectively superior."

Derek looked at Dirk, who shrugged. "Any topping fancier than pepperoni or sausage has ideas above its station."

Checking in! How harmonious are you?

The LitenVärld family believes that individual voices create the most beautiful music when singing together. A single off-key note can ruin the harmony, and that's never truer than when it comes to our special exempt employees.

If you're reading this, it's because someone has raised concerns about your performance that might suggest a potential discordance. This is nothing to worry about! Feedback is a necessary part of growth.

Please rate the following questions on a scale from one (this is not at all true for me) to five (I agree wholeheartedly and unambiguously).

EMOTIONAL HEALTH

1. I am happy and fulfilled in my work and life.
2. I relish the chance to do better at my job.
3. Most of my waking thoughts are devoted to improving the performance of my teammates and managers in any way I can.
4. My greatest ambition is to be an exemplary employee.
5. I do not dream. My mind is unclouded.

PHYSICAL HEALTH

1. I am in perfect physical health.

2. *My body does everything I or anyone else needs it to do.*
3. *I sleep well and wake refreshed, ready to start the day.*
4. *I have never experienced any of the following: illness, injury, hallucinations, phantom limb pain, personality changes, sudden hemorrhaging, or inexplicable subdermal growths.*

SELF-PERCEPTION

1. *I lack nothing.*
2. *I am grateful that I exist at all in this chaotic universe filled with random chance.*
3. *I am lucky. So lucky.*

If you find yourself answering anything below a 4 (strongly agree), and especially if you experience any signs of illness, injury, hallucinations, phantom limb pain, personality changes, sudden hemorrhaging, or inexplicable subdermal growths, call the following number immediately and await further instruction.

From *The LitenVärldSpecial Employee's Handbook*

Chapter 5

Expecting the Unexpected

The breakroom was too claustrophobic with all five of them, so they settled around a farmhouse-style table in a nearby showroom.

The team had been given a map of the store, but it was already out of date. The VIP lounge wasn't included, and the maskhål and Derek's encounter with the toilet had disrupted several showrooms.

"That fuckin' figures," Dex said grumpily. He was doodling something onto the scratched surface of the bench he and Delilah were sitting on. Derek frowned at him, but decided if it was anything *too* explicit or company-unfriendly, he'd clean it off later.

To his surprise, Dirk casually pulled the pen out of Dex's hand and hit him on the nose with it. It was an oddly immature move.

"What the fuck, man!" Dex spat, rubbing at his nose. "That hurt!"

"No destruction of company property except for defekta," Dirk said, and Derek felt himself nodding. "And watch the language. Resource Management has already flagged our team's unprofessional demeanor."

"I can talk however I—"

"Dex," Darkness hissed.

Dex shrank a little. There was a moment of awkward silence.

"I can correct it," Derek said, pulling out the pen he always carried with him alongside his wrench set. "The map. I know some shortcuts that wouldn't be recorded."

"Good, that's good, Derek," Dirk said. "Mark those on the map, if you don't mind."

Derek snuck looks at each of his team members while correcting their map. Delilah and Darkness spoke among themselves. Dirk paced back and forth, routinely checking each quadrant of the room, making sure no defekta had snuck up on them. Dex ran his fingers over the half-finished doodle, which seemed to be a stylized version of his own name, and a fairly artistic one.

He couldn't help seeing each of them through the lens of himself. Delilah channeled the calm and capability that Derek felt when completing familiar tasks, although she seemed alternately weary and harried. Dex boiled with the twitchy energy Derek felt when thrown into a new challenge or unfamiliar territory. He was constantly looking around, observing, taking the emotional temperature of the group—but where Derek would try and calm everyone, Dex seemed to enjoy poking and prying at the little cracks in people's moods.

When Derek looked at Darkness and Dirk, he saw only what he lacked. Derek lacked Darkness's directness, their nerve, and, seemingly, their comfort in their own skin. Darkness seemed to fill the spaces they occupied. Everything about them distracted him. It made Derek distinctly unsettled; he'd grown so used to staying in the background, trying to be invisible.

And Dirk ... Dirk was a leader. Dirk was the largest presence in the room, larger even than Darkness. Derek could feel the way everyone orbited around him, including Derek himself. Even when Dirk wasn't talking or looking at them, Dex, Delilah, and Darkness maintained a constant awareness of his presence.

Derek was good at watching and understanding the moods and dynamics of the people he encountered. It made him an excellent sales associate, but Derek was not a leader. He had never thought of himself as one, and felt relieved that he'd be able to follow someone else through the night.

He could see that the group had faults and fissures—which group didn't? Despite that, Derek couldn't help but think about how he could fit into their dynamic, maybe even improve it; bring Dex out of his shell a little, share Delilah's work so she wouldn't look so weighed down. Offer himself as a buffer for the odd tension between Dirk and Darkness.

"There," he said, finishing with the map. He flipped it around, presenting it to the rest of the inventory team.

Darkness sighed. "These layouts are all the same but changed just enough to disorient you. It's like déjà vu."

"The disorientation is by design," Dirk said, coming over and looking down at the map. Darkness and Delilah both silently moved out of his way, so he didn't have to loom over them, but he barely noticed. He traced his fingers through the store's veins and arteries, tapping on the secret throughways that Derek had marked in red. Dirk looked up from the map and met Derek's eyes in an unblinking gaze.

"This is good work," he said. "Thank you, Derek."

Derek flushed, equal parts pleased and uncomfortable with public praise. Tricia had very rarely offered any, and his coworkers barely acknowledged his presence.

"It should be easy to cover in teams," Dirk said. "Dex and Delilah on the north side, me and Derek on the south, then we'll tackle the VIP lounge as a team. Darkness can keep an eye on CCTV from the customer service desk and coordinate us, give us a heads up if that toilet drops stealth long enough to pin it down."

The other three Ds shared a look. "You wanna take the green kid with you?" Dex asked.

"He isn't even trained," Delilah added.

Darkness just shifted their gaze between Dirk and Derek, who was still blushing. He'd never really been chosen for a team like this before—only assigned. It felt very different.

"You learn best by doing," Dirk said, and Derek nodded. He'd found exactly the same thing to be true in his work.

"Sure, for like, arts and crafts," Darkness said, standing up. "Gotta make a mess with finger paints before you can paint *Starry Night* or whatever. Not with this."

"He evaded a level-four defekta with stealth capability until backup arrived. And now he'll have an INVENTERA of his own, and he'll be on comms," Dirk said calmly. Then he smirked—a strange expression to see on what was, essentially, Derek's own face. "You'll be able to swoop in and save him if it gets too scary."

The air between them was tense. Derek looked at Dex and Delilah to see their reactions, but they were both looking intently away; Dex was engrossed by his phone, and Delilah was checking her equipment with the same intensity.

"I don't need protection," Derek said. The two of them looked over at him; Dirk with a considering look, Darkness with a trace of pity. The latter irritated him enough that he repeated himself. "I don't need it, and I don't want it. I want to help. I'd be proud to help."

Darkness's jaw clenched. "Well, far be it from me to suppress your LitenVärld spirit."

He didn't understand Darkness's bitterness, and it hurt to have it aimed at him.

"I thought you'd be happy to coordinate comms," Dirk said to Darkness. His voice was flat, but there was a subtle undertone of mockery. "You do love the sound of your own voice."

There was a thunk from the table. Dex had slapped his hand down on the scratched finish. "Are you all done with this pissing contest? Thought we were on a schedule."

Darkness grinned at that, Dirk rolled his eyes, and the tension between them seemed to collapse. The five of them divided up the rooms, with Darkness barricaded at the customer service desk in the center of the sales floor. Dex and Delilah would take the kitchens, bathrooms, and children's sections. Derek and Dirk would tackle the northern end of the store, which held the bedrooms, living areas, and backyards and recreation. The VIP area was right in the center, not far from the customer service desk, and they would take that on as a full team.

"Once we're there, we'll figure out a strategy to flush out the toilet from . . . what?" Dirk said irritably. Dex had snorted in laughter. When Derek looked over, Darkness was grinning, and Delilah was trying very hard to keep a straight face.

"What?" Dirk said again.

Delilah, not quite able to keep the amusement off her face, asked, "Your plan is to flush the toilet?"

Dex's snort was loud this time, and Darkness threw their head back and laughed. Derek smiled too—it was such a stupid joke, but it was funny, and it was nice to see a joke played so harmlessly at someone else's expense.

"Oh, ha *ha,*" Dirk said sourly. "I can't believe you're all older than me and still haven't grown the hell up."

Derek wiped the smile off his face and looked down before Dirk noticed, but couldn't quite stop his lips from twitching when Darkness said in a not-really-undertone, "Guess we have proof that a sense of humor isn't genetic."

• • •

The five of them traveled as a pack to the customer service desk first, with three people setting up Darkness's communications and surveillance hub, while the other two kept watch.

Derek felt nervous around Dex. Part of it was due to residual anxiety and wariness around all teenagers, who seemed to sense Derek's innate love for rules and authority, and either mercilessly made fun of him for it or avoided him altogether.

But Dex wasn't any teenager. He wasn't a coworker or customer—he *was* Derek, or rather, they were both something made from the same source material. Derek wanted to believe this gave them some sort of connection that they could build a foundation on.

And since Derek was technically the adult, it was up to him to lay the first brick.

"Whatcha doing?" he asked, squatting down next to Dex, who was holding a phone a few inches from his face and typing sullenly into it.

Dex slowly turned his gaze up to Derek without moving his head, eyebrows tilted in a disbelieving gaze. "Posting a SnapYap," he said drily.

"Oh, that's cool!" Derek said. "I love SnapYap."

Dex regarded him warily. "You know what it is?"

Derek nodded eagerly. He had helped maintain the store's social media in the weeks before Christmas, since nobody else was interested or willing to take it on. He had carefully researched best practices, brainstormed different aesthetic and rhetorical approaches, and kept careful notes on engagement so he could send Tricia weekly summaries of their analytics. And in his off hours, he had ended up using the app as a blunt weapon to beat back the loneliness that haunted his nights and mornings; watching endless videos of porch container gardeners in Brooklyn or the daily trials of twentysomethings living out of a van in the Yucatán Peninsula. It had been a great distraction, until LitenVärld had decided to consolidate all social media accounts under the main corporate office's control.

"Did you ever see the Unlikely Umbrellas account?" Derek asked.

Dex's stare shifted in intensity, from wary hostility to passionate fervor. "I fucking *love* Unlikely Umbrellas," he said. "Do you know Only Good Dogs? I chatted with the girl that runs it, she gave me all this awesome advice about running an account."

"Really? How cool." Derek had never heard of the account, but if it featured only good dogs, it was probably great.

There was a disgusted scoff from behind them. "Great, this team needed another wannabe *influencer*," said Dirk, imbuing the last word with an acidic disdain.

Derek shrank from his disappointment, quickly trying to explain himself. "I mostly used SnapYap to help out the store." Dirk looked mollified, so Derek added, "I just think it's a great platform to connect to our quirky customer base."

"That's good," Dirk nodded approvingly. "I'm glad to know

some people have their priorities straight."

The praise did not make Derek feel very good, since it came at the expense of Dex going utterly stone-faced. Once Dirk had wandered back to do a final equipment check, Dex yanked his phone back out, typing furiously into it. Once he was done, he leaned back a little. Derek was unable to stop himself from sneaking a peek.

The post was an unflattering up-angle selfie of Dex's glaring face, along with the words, MY FACE WHEN MY COWORKER NARCS ON ME FOR USING SNAPYAP THEN LOOKS OVER MY SHOULDER TO SEE WHAT I'M POSTING

FUCK YOU DEREK U NARC #HATEMYJOB #KILL-MENOW

• • •

Dirk and Derek made their way back to the northern end of the store, while Darkness, Delilah, and Dex went south. The three of them gave him odd looks before they left; slightly wary, maybe a little sympathetic. It was too similar to how his normal coworkers looked at him. He felt as if he had somehow been put into place, written off. Just Derek being Derek.

Dirk must have sensed the shift in his mood as the other three left, because he clapped him on the shoulder again. "You ready for this?" he asked, but then didn't wait for an answer. "Of course you are. You were born ready for this."

He pulled out one of the INVENTERA scanner guns, holding it out handle-first to Derek. When Derek hesitated, unable to forget its violent whine when it was shot over his head, Dirk pushed it, gently but insistently, into his hand.

"You were *made* for this," Dirk said. "You don't have to pretend to be meek and mild right now. Stop analyzing every situation and trying to figure out how to please everyone."

He grinned, and Derek couldn't seem to look away. So strong, fierce, independent; as if Dirk had been freed from all the turmoil and loneliness that Derek could never seem to shake.

"Do you trust me?" Dirk asked intently.

"I trust you," Derek said, though that wasn't quite true; he didn't trust himself, and Dirk seemed like a version of himself that was too good to be true.

But he wanted to believe Dirk, in what his existence seemed to promise. So he took the INVENTERA.

"It's . . . light," he said, surprised. He shouldn't be; he'd carried the entire box of them upstairs, but in his hand, it felt lighter even than plastic. Its black sheen seemed slightly iridescent in the yellow emergency lights. It reminded him of a beetle's carapace.

"I know," Dirk said. "They're perfect tools for the job. Just like us."

He whipped his own out, swinging it around the room to aim it at an end table. "They're lightweight, intuitive to use, almost impossible to break—you really have to stomp the heck out of one to crack the casing. They can't hurt anything except defekta, so there's no danger of friendly fire, no collateral damage to the stores. They send out clean energetic pulses that target the mutagenic agents and render them inert."

The scanner beeped, and a small flood of information filled the screen.

Derek had leaned close into Dirk to read it, and he was aware, like with Darkness, of the other person's nearness.

Darkness had felt warm, their touch soft and careful. Dirk's presence was a little more electric, like the air around him was charged, crackling.

Dirk tapped the big red X at the top of the screen. "That means it's safe. For now, anyway. So for now, we move on."

Derek was able to intuit the rest of the process himself, troubleshooting as he went and solving problems with minimal effort. Dirk didn't praise him again, but he did notice, and never hesitated to give him a proud nod. It didn't feel patronizing or forced, the way Tricia often did when complimenting a worker's performance. The brief acknowledgment made him feel warmer than any coupon for a free day-old pastry—Tricia's normal reward for being the top-rated sales associate in their weekly survey results.

Almost despite himself, Derek fell into a fantasy of joining the inventory team, taking on special inventories across Liten-Värld's networks. Derek liked being busy, liked exacting tasks that were detail-rich but not complex. In some ways, it was disappointing to know that he'd been created for this kind of work. But it made a huge difference, knowing that all of the things that others treated as idiosyncrasies, or worse, helped him serve a purpose. Seeing Dirk perform the same behaviors and tics that had always set Derek apart—shifting his weight back and forth when he was excited, hyperfocusing on a single task, even the way he frequently blinked, which at least one coworker had told Derek was weird and distracting—was enormously validating. He'd felt so anomalous and so lonely. Maybe he was still an anomaly, but he was no longer alone.

They had cleared three rooms with no defekta when Derek's INVENTERA gave a warbling trill. The room they were in was styled after a Victorian garden; Astroturf under their feet, faux-stone arches wound with heavy plastic flowers, wicker chairs, and a croquet set. Derek's INVENTERA had been focused on a table made of glass and baroque wrought iron. Its legs curved toward the floor in elongated spirals, and the glass top of the table nestled into a wrought iron oval with stylized roses and ivy worked into a pattern.

Derek looked closer at the readout—they really should have made the text bigger on the interface, especially since he didn't have the enhanced vision that the rest of the group did.

- EXF-23301-01
- NAV: 2241
- GEN: 2.3.100
- STATUS: **DEFEKT**
- DISCONTINUE IMMEDIATELY

Dirk's head had snapped up at the sound. "Derek. Step back slowly."

Derek looked back at the table only to see it staring up at him. Some of the wrought iron roses along the side had blinked open, and half a dozen eyes with silvery irises were now focused on him.

"Okay," Derek said, remembering how the SVINLÅDA had been calm at first, so long as he was. He put up one of his hands, and a couple of the eyes followed it calmly. One of the legs unfurled curiously out to him, reaching for his hand as if it wanted to touch him.

"Nothing to worry about, right?" he said. "We're calm."

There was another warbling tune from behind him, and then that terrible, grating mosquito whine. Derek could feel it this time as well, a blistering heat that cut through the air inches from his palm. Dirk's aim was impeccable, and the table's outstretched leg shattered into sharp metal spikes and a spray of sky-blue liquid that Derek realized was probably blood. The table let out a ringing, metallic cry and staggered back on its three remaining legs. It tried to flee, knocking over wicker furniture and tearing into the Astroturf. Dirk walked up, unhurried but completely focused, aiming his INVENTERA at the table and squeezing off another shot. This one hit a second leg, and the table collapsed. Its cries grew shriller.

Dirk shouldered him aside—not angrily, barely even cognizant of Derek standing there. Derek stumbled back.

It gave him a perfect view as Dirk blew a third leg off the table. Its scream petered out, breaking into a series of hushed whimpers. The table tried desperately to pull itself away with its one remaining leg, the rest of its jagged stumps twitching in agony, sluggishly leaking bright blue blood into the Astroturf.

Stop, Derek wanted to scream, but his teeth were clenched so hard that he heard the enamel squeak inside his skull. *Stop hurting it.*

Dirk looked curiously over his shoulder at Derek. The fact that their faces were almost the same was horrible now; Dirk's face was splashed with the thing's blood, and his eyes held no remorse or consternation. The table gave another weak little cry, and Dirk's face twitched in annoyance. He turned back and shot the table again, this time in the center of its glass top. It immediately went limp and collapsed. Some of the eyes looked around and found Derek, focusing on him. He couldn't look away.

There was no clear line between when the eyes belonged to

Quarterly Performance Review

Employee number: D-64598-01-6-13-150
Designation: Dirk
Division and position: Inventera/Team Lead

Description of role and responsibilities:

I lead the remaining Inventera Team in LitenVärld's ongoing efforts to contain and exterminate its defective products. During each shift, I decide our strategy and coordinate our actions, while also eliminating defekta. I motivate my team members, develop our strengths while also identifying areas of improvement, and mediate conflicts that arise both during stressful shifts and in our off time. I also work closely with my superiors at Resource Management to set goals and evaluate our team's progress.

Discuss areas of excellence in your work:

I am an excellent leader. I lead by example. I get things done. I'm not afraid to do what it takes to succeed. I have high expectations and don't hesitate to tell people when they fall short of them. I thrive under pressure, and I perform very well in stressful situations. I'm not afraid to speak my mind. I am extremely loyal to LitenVärld and grateful that I've been given the opportunity to elevate myself to something better.

Discuss areas to improve:

After talking with Reagan, I understand that I need to work on my listening and communication skills.

Comments from reviewer:

Dirk has proven to be the shake-up that the Inventera Division needed! His team has been smashing through every goal we set for them and exceeding all their quotas, which proves his skill at motivating others. He's also a delight to work with: quick, responsive, and a real go-getter. We discussed developing a more open communication style with his team, and he was very receptive to feedback. I'll be talking with the rest of his team about strategies to collectively resolve conflict, rather than needing managers to intervene over every little thing. Overall, Dirk's been an amazing addition!
—*Reagan*

From LitenVärld's Employee Files, Inventera Division

Chapter 6

There Is No Escape . . . From Fun!

It took a while for Derek to become aware of Dirk snapping his fingers in his face. Derek jerked away, gasping harshly.

"Hey, you back with me?" Dirk asked.

"What the hell was that?"

"Defekta." Dirk said it without any kind of inflection or emotion. "You can't just wait for them to attack you. You have to show initiative."

Derek had a flashback to watching Tricia train new temps on engaging with customers: *You can't just wait for them to notice you. You have to show initiative and approach them first.*

Derek shook his head. "Wh . . . What happened to the IN-VENTERA targeting the mutagenic gene and rendering it inert?"

Dirk looked over his shoulder at the dead, shattered table. "Looks pretty inert to me."

Rage and adrenaline flooded through him, and Derek balled up his fists, wanting to smash them into Dirk's face, which now looked *monstrous* to him, all the more so because it shared Derek's features. Dirk looked back at him calmly, commanding and unconcerned.

"This is the job we were given," Dirk said, gazing unblinkingly into Derek's eyes. "This is the purpose we were made for.

You going to fight against that?"

Derek wanted to, at least for a second. Then he realized how futile it would be; fighting Dirk would be like fighting a better, cooler, and crueler version of himself. And fighting Liten-Värld? It seemed more than impossible; it was unthinkable.

Derek dropped his gaze and bit down on the answer (*yes, I will fight it, I must*) that threatened to erupt out of him. Pain tore through his throat again, so sudden and wrenching that he choked, tears springing to his eyes.

"Wow, they really did a number on your generation, huh?" Dirk said, disgust and disappointment edging into his voice. "I'd heard they were trying to make the sevens empathetic or something, but it looks like they went too far. I hope you're good for more than calming down suburbanites, otherwise this is going to be a long night for both of us."

He stood up, stretching. "I'm here to work, you know? Not babysit. I take my job very seriously."

There was a chime from Derek's earpiece.

"I heard screaming," Delilah said, her voice tinny in the speaker. "Do you guys need help?"

Dirk sighed and unmuted his earpiece. "Derek met his first defekta. Well, his second, I guess. It got a little messy, but we're okay."

"Derek?" Delilah said. "What's your status?"

Derek could feel the ache settle back into his throat. He could feel Dirk staring down at him, waiting to see how he'd react. He tried to clear his throat. "I'm okay. Just . . . it was a lot."

The silence in his earpiece was hard to read. "Are you good to keep going?" Delilah asked.

"Of cour—" Derek tried to say, but felt something squirm rebelliously in his throat, worse than it had been since he called in sick. He tried to cover it with a cough, still aware of Dirk's scrutiny and hesitant to let him down. "Sorry," he said hoarsely. "I'll be fine."

"Okay," Delilah said. "Dex and I cleared our quadrant. We'll keep going."

"Got it, so will we." Dirk muted his earpiece and looked expectantly at Derek. His finger was still around the trigger of the INVENTERA. "Well? Are you good?"

Derek recognized his tone as the one he used on strangers, new coworkers and customers. It was cheerful, smooth, and gave absolutely nothing away. He smiled back at Dirk, ignored the swelling ache in his throat, and replied with the same. "Yeah, I'm just gonna, you know. Shake it off and get ready for the next one."

Dirk's smile curved up into something a little realer. "Good, Derek. That's good to hear."

• • •

Derek knew about praying. Several of his Muslim coworkers scheduled their breaks around daily prayers. The store attracted its share of evangelical customers who asked about his relationship with his personal savior, inquiring into the state of his soul. His answers unnerved them enough that his coworkers had taken to calling him over to handle anyone attempting to debate Zahra about her hijab.

He had never prayed himself, never given any thought to gods. There was already a higher power in his life, and it was LitenVärld. Any and all acts of devotion were for its favor, rather than an intangible presence that he couldn't comprehend.

Now, though, he found himself swallowing a litany of pleas: *Please let this room be empty, please let me not find another defekta, please let them stay hidden, please get them out of here.* He prayed that the defekta would sense Dirk's menace, the violence that lurked beneath his placid face, and make their way to other rooms.

Derek's throat *throbbed* with all the words he didn't dare say.

Maybe his prayers were heard. They went through showroom after showroom, from a dining room styled like a pseudo-Asian teahouse to a minimalist urban loft with fake exposed brick, but each of them was clear of defekta. There were empty spaces where Derek knew furnishings had been; the arc lamp that hung over the black oak desk in the minimalist loft was no longer there, and a green-felted mahjong table was missing from the teahouse. Dirk kicked the tiles that had been left scattered across the ground with suspicion, but Derek could only shrug.

"The closing crews aren't reliable," he said. "You saw the dirty mugs in the breakroom sink."

They had nearly finished the second quadrant when Derek heard a familiar scraping noise, and felt the bottom fall out of his stomach.

Dirk held up a fist, signaling Derek to stop. He swiveled his head, trying to pinpoint the noise, while Derek prayed, again, *Don't move, stop moving, please.*

"Shut *up*, Derek!" Dirk said. "Quit fucking *muttering* to yourself!"

Derek went silent. Even his thoughts cut out, the babbling monologue that he had somehow unintentionally given voice. He very carefully kept his mind clear as he followed Dirk into the room—an open-floor living room and kitchen combo with a mid-aughts's kawaii aesthetic: pastels, a plum-colored couch decorated with throw pillows in the shapes of strawberries and cartoony cat plushies, stoneware featuring popular anime characters.

The upside-down wicker basket stood out starkly to Derek's eye, but he busied himself looking everywhere else. He turned his INVENTERA on the kitchenette first, keeping Dirk in the corner of his eye.

Dirk was scanning methodically through the living room. The lack of action over the previous hour seemed to have worn on his nerves; he was no longer being careful to leave the room in customer-ready shape. Instead he threw items onto the ground after he scanned them, leaving a trail of plushie fruit and baked goods. Derek edged closer to the wicker basket, trying to keep his head utterly empty of words, casually scanning items to look busy. LYKKE chair, LYKKE chair, sloth-shaped fruit bowl, table runner embroidered with fat cats—

Derek froze when his INVENTERA warbled again. In his peripheral vision, he could see Dirk pivot toward him, INVENTERA raised and finger cocked on its trigger.

He barely had time to react before the table runner leapt at him. It wrapped itself around his arm—the tassels on each end were tipped in curved, needle-thin claws, and Derek could feel them pricking into his uniform.

He felt the INVENTERA's whine this time, felt the pulse of energy impact the table runner and then, horribly, pass through it. The energy was as invasive as its sound, and it hurt far worse than the claws, burning his skin under his uniform.

The table runner was still trying to squeeze weakly around his wrist, as if for comfort. He could taste something thick and coppery in his mouth.

"I'm sorry," he said—sobbed, really.

He heard it this time; the other voice, *his* other voice, repeating the same words. *I'm sorry. I'm sorry. I'm sorry.*

Dirk yanked the table runner out of his hand, threw it on the ground, and shot it again. Then he turned to stare at Derek.

"What the hell is wrong with you?" he demanded. His tone was lower than Derek's, who tended to pitch his voice high and obsequious. Dirk's tone was angry, its authority absolute.

Derek folded under it like wet cardboard. "I just, it startled me, and I didn't, I couldn't aim without hitting myself—"

"No, what's *wrong with you*," Dirk repeated. He was still holding the INVENTERA out, and it was not pointed at the crumpled, stained table runner on the ground. It was pointed at Derek.

Derek tried to keep that blankness at the forefront of his mind, thick enough to gag the other voice that kept speaking through him, and slowly raised his hands.

There was a chime in his earpiece, and then Darkness's voice. "Dirk, Derek, what the hell is happening? Why the fuck—"

Dirk impatiently unmuted himself: "Would you shut *up* for once in your life, I'm trying to do my *job*, unlike the rest of you."

Then he yanked off the earpiece, still staring daggers at Derek.

Derek could hear Darkness in his ear, cursing at Dirk. He didn't dare move his hands to unmute himself, or give any sign that he could hear them. "Derek, if you can still hear me—fuck. Try and calm him down, okay? Keep him talking until one of us can get there. He's dangerous, even if the IN-

VENTERA can't hurt you."

Derek swallowed. The INVENTERA *could* hurt him; the pulsing sheet of pain on his wrists told him that much. Dirk must have realized it as well.

Derek had dealt with angry customers before. None of them had ever pointed a weapon at him, but he'd been trained to handle emergencies. Well, he'd sat through a video. Parts of one, anyway, before Tricia had told him he was needed out on the sales floor.

Derek licked his lips, tried not to cringe at the thick, coppery blood that had been sprayed up into his face, and thought very hard.

A human touch in their time of need. What did Dirk need? Dirk needed to be understood, Derek thought. No, he needed to be respected.

"I can see that you're frustrated with my performance, Dirk, and I understand that—"

"Shut up, Derek. I know what you're doing," he said. "I am *literally* you, an earlier version of you. You're not going to customer-service your way out of this."

Dirk was so focused on Derek that he didn't notice the wicker basket inching closer to him. Derek tried to stop noticing it as well.

"What do you think *this* is then, Dirk?" It was important to use customers' names, if they gave them—it made them feel heard and recognized. Where had Derek learned that? Had it been in a training video? Had it been during *orientation,* which he had no real memory of? "Tell me what's wrong. Talk to me. I'm just trying to understand so I can do better."

"Something is wrong with *you*," Dirk said. "I thought you were just weak at first, that there was a flaw in your design that could be corrected. But it's not that, is it? You're like them."

Dirk gestured at the crumpled table runner on the ground between them.

"They're not even really alive. They're just . . . flukes. Accidents. Defectives. They're bugs that sneak into the system, and if we don't *fix* them, the system is in danger of breaking down."

Derek nodded mindlessly along with Dirk's bullshit, trying not to watch the wicker basket sneaking closer. "Dirk, thank you for telling me that, and I want you to know that I hear you. But have you considered that letting the defekta go *wouldn't* be a total disaster?"

Dirk's expression shifted, from anger into sharp exasperation, like he couldn't believe Derek was that stupid.

Derek could feel his voice threatening to break again. Words were thrumming in his throat: *Keep talking to me, Dirk.* "I just think that maybe you're catastrophizing a little—"

"You have no idea, do you?" Dirk said. "The only way for someone—for some*thing* like us to get ahead is to stand out. To be the best at what we're created to do. We were made to follow orders and anticipate needs, to know what had to be done before the orders were even conceived. If I stay ahead of that curve, then I . . ."

Dirk wanted power, Derek realized. Not respect. He didn't want to lead or be part of a team; he wanted control, and there wasn't much he wouldn't do to get it. He hadn't shown an ounce of squeamishness when killing the defekta, and Derek didn't think he himself would rate much more.

"Oh, you are good," Dirk said. He smiled bleakly at Derek. "You managed to get me monologuing. I guess I shouldn't be surprised."

The wicker basket settled a few inches behind Dirk's heels,

and Derek realized what the SVINLÅDA wanted him to do, a series of flashes that were strange enough for him to realize that they hadn't originated in his own mind.

Derek pushed a little of that desperation out, the way he had earlier when he'd broadcasted some telepathic warning signal to the other defekta. Derek had no idea if it worked the same way on a human, but it wouldn't hurt to try. *"Behind you!"*

It seemed to happen in slow motion, the moment when Dirk believed him enough to look. His head moved first, jerking backward over his shoulder, and when he didn't see anything, he shifted his weight and went to take a step back.

He knocked into the wicker basket, which was only a few inches below his knees. Just enough to unbalance him and move the INVENTERA's sights to Derek's left. Derek slapped the gun even further away, then shoved Dirk hard in the chest, sending him toppling over the basket, which went flying.

Derek snatched up the suddenly exposed SVINLÅDA and ran for it, ducking around the corner and sprinting, for the second time that night, down one of the twisting walkways that meandered through the sales floor.

There was a chime in his ear, and then Darkness's voice. "Derek? Can you make it to the customer service desk? I don't know what Dirk's—"

Their panicked voice was cut off. The SVINLÅDA had reached one pincered arm forward and plucked the earpiece out. After a momentary examination, it stuck it in the open cavern of their chest, muffling Darkness's voice.

"What are you—"

The SVINLÅDA pinched his arm, and Derek dropped it onto the ground with a clatter. It started racing ahead, clacking at Derek impatiently as if to hurry him on. It had apparently, at some point, grown an extra set of legs, and was moving fast.

Derek followed the SVINLÅDA through a series of rooms, through shortcuts Derek hadn't even known about, until they landed in a smaller one-room showroom, a tiny house set up with a nomadic chic atmosphere. The SVINLÅDA leapt up onto a sleeper sofa that had been left unfolded.

"What are you doing?" Derek hissed. He could hear footsteps growing closer.

The SVINLÅDA patted the thin mattress with its claw, like it was inviting Derek to have a friendly chat, or coaxing a twitchy cat to sit next to it.

Derek sat. He tried to leap back up as the sleeper sofa folded up over his legs. Before he could pull himself free, the sofa had drawn him back into itself, pressing over him in a way that was claustrophobic, distinctly uncomfortable, but not actually suffocating. The sofa seemed to sense his fear, and rumbled gently against Derek at a soothing frequency, a sub-audible purr. Almost despite himself, Derek began to calm.

The footsteps approached at an enraged clip. The sofa had silenced itself, and Derek held his breath. Dirk's footsteps paused for one heart-stopping, silent moment, and then moved on.

Derek let out a wheezing breath of relief.

After a moment, the sofa silently unfolded, and Derek wriggled free of its embrace. He looked from the sofa to the SVINLÅDA. "Thank you," he whispered.

The SVINLÅDA tiptoed next to Derek, reaching its spindly arms up to him. Derek held still as it touched its little pincers to his face—where the table runner's blood had splattered on him.

"Oh, I'm fine. It's . . . it's not my blood."

The SVINLÅDA seemed to shrink a little, retracting its arms back into the little drawers on its side. The sofa wheezed sadly.

"I'm sorry," he said. "I didn't—"

He'd been about to say, *I didn't know,* but ignorance couldn't excuse this. He'd joined a team to exterminate them.

"I'm sorry," he repeated. "I wish I could stop them, but I think it would be easier if we . . . if we ran away."

He could hear the doubt laced through his voice. Once the words left his mouth, he had to consider the fact that while he had a near-encyclopedic knowledge of interior design trends, furniture assembly, and customer service, he had almost no idea what *away* encompassed. He couldn't remember ever leaving LitenVärld's parking lot or looking beyond the surrounding fields where his container sat.

Still, he was fairly sure that *away* contained a non-zero chance of him surviving the night, which became more doubtful every moment he spent inside LitenVärld.

Derek could just barely hear a muffled chime from inside the SVINLÅDA. It opened up its chest and extracted the earpiece. He took it and stuck it back in his ear, shooting a quick look around before unmuting it.

"Derek?" Darkness said. "Can you hear me?"

"Yeah," he whispered.

"Good," they said. "Now *what the fuck is going on*?"

"Where's Dirk?"

"Heading into the children's section. He'll probably circle back my way in a sec. Can you get out of sight of the cameras?"

"Downstairs in receiving and assembly. Those camera feeds are only accessible from the manager's office."

"Good enough," Darkness said. "Be quick, I'll try to meet you down there."

He nodded, then muted the earpiece again.

"If I can get the delivery doors open down in assembly," he whispered to the sofa, "you can take the cargo elevator down, and we'll escape through there."

If he couldn't imagine a life outside LitenVärld, he had no idea what a sofa would do. Maybe they could go to the Goodwill down the road? Did other employers let their workers live onsite? Derek wondered if that explained the strange looks he'd gotten when he mentioned living in one of the empty cargo boxes in the back parking lot.

Disciplinary Report
Employee number: D-64598-01-2-45-100
Designation: Dex
This is a:
( ) Step One
( ) Step Two
(✓) Step Three
( ) Termination Level Offense (please check one)

Please describe the infraction:

I hate everything about this job except for my teammates, so I ran away and lived in an abandoned El Buckarito for a week. When you assholes came to drag me back, I broke at least one person's nose and made you chase me into a swamp. Then I sang Queen's "We Are the Champions" as loud as I could on the drive back to HQ, over and over. Nobody but me appreciated it, so I guess I need to practice more.

Managers: please describe the disciplinary action taken at this time (check all that apply):

- *Verbal warning*
- *Written warning ✓*
- *Change or reduction in wages*

○ description:

- Change or reduction in duties

  ○ description:

- Change in team structure ✓

  ○ description: We will be moving forward with restructuring the Inventera Division, due to high attrition, low quality of work, and persistent attitude problems among the remaining team, as demonstrated here. Our next phase will concentrate on fostering better discipline and internal regulation, and incentivizing higher standards of work. Dex has been made to understand how his actions have sped up our decision to move forward with this restructuring.

- Forced isolation/suspension ✓
- Public apology and recantation ✓
- Participatory shaming
- Corporal punishment

  ○ description:

- Termination and/or discontinuation

Do I feel as if I adequately understand the severity of my infraction:
Fuck you.
Do I feel as if this punishment fits my infraction:

FUCK you.

Do I understand that under LitenVärld's progressive disciplinary process, I will face increasingly severe punishments, up to and including termination and/or discontinuation? And that progressive disciplinary process may be skipped in the face of particularly egregious infractions?

I fucking look forward to it. (Also FUCK YOU!!!)

From LitenVärld's Employee Files, Inventera Division

Chapter 7

When "Don't Be Evil" Fails,
Try "Don't Be Boring"

As he made his way down to receiving and assembly, Derek felt every doubt that flooded into his brain weighing on him. He'd never been a leader; he had literally been designed to follow orders. He had no power here, no weapon, and since Dirk must have told the others that he was a defekta, no other allies beyond a sofa and a toy chest shaped like a pig-crab. What if his memory was faulty, and everything he knew about the locations of the security footage was wrong?

He was so *stupid*. Why had he thought he could do this?

Oddly, it was Darkness's words that came back to him; he knew exactly what he'd been made for, but he could choose what he *wanted* to be. He couldn't go back to who he had been two days ago, the Sales Associate of the Month with a 4.74 customer satisfaction rating, the employee who lived and breathed the LitenVärld ethos. He was discordant, defective, but he'd already known that, hadn't he? In the great, humming machine of LitenVärld, he'd always felt misaligned and out of step. Even before he knew the truth, he'd known that much. Now he had a choice.

Derek felt the bandage over his throat as he slipped through the showrooms, making his way quietly to the spiral staircase that led downstairs to receiving and assembly. The pain had stopped when he'd gotten away from Dirk, but the bandage was itching like crazy. He paused long enough to roll down the collar of his turtleneck, dig his thumbnail under the corner of the adhesive, and peel it off.

The next moment was like his mental sinuses cleared. The same way he had broadcasted his prayers to both the other defekta and Dirk, when he focused on *listening,* it felt like his nerves extended far outside his body, past the normal range of his senses. He could hear Dirk's furious footsteps stalking back north, back toward the customer service desk, where Darkness was pacing back and forth. Two sets of lighter footsteps that Derek identified as Dex and Delilah were moving toward the central hub of the sales floor. The sleeper sofa and the SVIN-LÅDA were making their cautious way to the cargo elevators, keeping to the fringes of the showrooms.

But he could hear more; dozens and dozens of defekta in hiding, stealthily moving through the store on their impossible appendages. They were slipping through the shortcuts between rooms, curling through gaps between the modular walls or just silently unbolting them, moving them around.

Stay safe, Derek thought. *Stay hidden.*

A ripple of acknowledgment made its way back to him.

The tight spiral staircase that led down to receiving and assembly was hidden behind the false wall in the Hipster Nursery, with its mural of ironically ugly cartoon monsters. It was only for employees, and like everything out of the public eye, was aesthetically awful and liberally interpreted the safety code. Derek slipped carefully down it, wary of every squeak and rattle. He paused at the bottom, long enough to sigh and rest his head against the wall. He'd made it this far. He was leaving. And he'd get two of the defekta out with him.

His earpiece chimed, startling him. Derek flinched, then unmuted it, but didn't say anything, still too jumpy.

"I managed to convince Dirk that you've avoided all the CCTV cameras, and we're all splitting up to hunt you down," said Darkness.

It took Derek a few seconds to find his voice. "Is that supposed to be comforting?"

"I'm on my way to you," Darkness said. That wasn't an answer, Derek noted. "I'll be there as soon as I find my way through these fucking showrooms. I swear, they keep changing when I'm not looking."

Derek muted the earpiece again. He thought about running now, asking the defekta to lead Darkness away from him, buy him enough time to run for it.

But the SVINLÅDA and the sofa were still making their circuitous route down to assembly. He'd promised to get them out as well.

And he *wanted* to trust Darkness. He didn't want to be alone. He felt a bond with the defekta, but the belonging he'd felt—or at least the potential to belong—when surrounded by people who understood him down to his DNA was too much to give up. The memory of that feeling held him in place.

If only Darkness's and Dirk's footsteps didn't sound so similar.

Derek lost his nerve, retreating back amid the tall shelves. He wished miserably for a weapon, or that he'd taken his chance to run; this felt too much like getting drawn into a trap. Darkness came down the stairs slowly, cautiously. The INVENTERA wasn't in their hand, but within easy reach in the holster strapped around their thigh. Derek's nerves crackled with remembered pain.

"Derek?" they whispered.

"I'm here," he said. *Don't come closer,* he thought. The fear felt like it was lashing out of him.

Darkness winced. "Oh, that is weird. I'm just gonna get off the stairs, okay? Feels like this whole thing'll drop if I lean on it wrong."

They waited, and Derek realized they were asking for his permission to come any closer. He tried to calm down a little. "Okay," he said. "You can come down."

As they did, he moved a little further back. He lost sight of Darkness, but all of his senses still bent toward them, focusing on the creaking leather of combat boots, the rustle of heavy-duty twill, the faintest sub-audible whine from their INVEN-TERA, the smell of sweat and pine-scented deodorant—

"I really thought Dirk was bullshitting us," said Darkness. Their steps were soft as they came off the stairs and onto the concrete. "He said when you spoke it was like someone scratching words right into his brain."

Derek retreated further back into the shadows of the room. "I didn't even know it was happening until he yelled at me about it."

"He said you were defective. Not just discordant, but . . ." Darkness trailed off.

But what? thought Derek.

"But you still seem like one of us," Darkness said.

Derek bit his lip, feeling a pathetic thrill at being included in any kind of *us.* "It's my throat. There was something weird in it. Then it was outside of it, too."

Darkness mulled this over. "The bandage on your neck. You didn't cut yourself?"

He hadn't cut himself. He hadn't hallucinated the feeling of something opening in his throat. It felt like a relief to finally admit it to himself. Something was wrong with him. "It just opened up," he explained. "And any time I said something just because someone wanted to hear it, it *hurt*—"

"This is so fucking weird," Darkness said, putting a hand to their head. "It's like it's resonating, somehow. I can see why Dirk called it hypnotizing, but I'm pretty sure that's because he's a sociopath who doesn't believe other beings actually have feelings."

They started to take another step forward, then hesitated. "Can I come closer?" they asked.

Derek could still hear the mosquito whine of the INVENTERA on their hip. "Could you," he asked, then faltered. What if this was what made them turn on him? "Can you put your gun away? The INVENTERA."

They unstrapped it from their hip and tossed it carelessly into one of the oversized garbage cans. "If you *do* hypnotize me, please make me do weird and horny things."

"I'm not—I wouldn't—!"

Derek could hear the grin in their voice. "I know, Derek. Might be fun to try sometime, though."

Darkness rounded the corner of the aisle he had been hiding in, spotting him crouched behind a tower of boxes. They approached with their hands up, like Derek was a wounded animal. He supposed he was: his throat felt a little better, but his arms throbbed from the table runner's claws and the INVENTERA's shots.

His new senses lit up at Darkness's approach; he could feel the tremors in their fingers, betraying their nerves, the way the air stirred at their breath, even the heat that their skin gave off.

"Can I see it?" they asked. "Your throat."

Derek felt a prickly heat along his limbs, embarrassment mixing with the same touch-hunger he'd felt when Darkness had checked him for a concussion. He was still trying to understand the unfamiliar shape of *wanting*. He wasn't practiced in it, since his material needs were all met.

(Weren't they? Derek thought of how often he'd awoken feeling crushed under the weight of his own solitude, and wondered.)

"Sure," he said hoarsely. "If you—I don't mind."

Darkness smiled slowly at him. "Wow. You really can't control it—the broadcasting, I mean."

Derek groaned, but let Darkness steer him down to sit on a pallet of shelving units.

They glanced up as they crouched, and Derek flushed even more, mortified by everything he was feeling and undoubtedly—what had Darkness called it?—*broadcasting*. But Darkness's smile was friendly, understanding.

Darkness gently pushed Derek's jaw up, tilting his head back and exposing his neck. Derek swallowed convulsively as Darkness rolled down the collar of his turtleneck, their fingers soft as they brushed against his flushed skin.

Derek had never considered himself desirable. If asked about his best qualities, he would have said that he was a hard worker, a good listener, reliable, organized. His body was made to be useful: to assemble furniture and flatpacks, to ring up customers, to go and do and be anything that was asked of it. His pleasure came from the completion of a task, a job well done. It didn't come from his body, just what his body could do in service.

So he had no frame of reference for what he felt, being touched like this.

"Should I stop?" they asked. Their fingers were warm against his sweaty neck. Their hands were nearly the same as Derek's, besides the smudged black marker ink on their fingernails.

Derek shook his head. He wanted them to see it; needed *someone* to see it, to witness it, to confirm he wasn't imagining it. That the defect was real, was part of him.

"Wow," Darkness said. They leaned a little closer. "Oh, wow. That's—"

"What?" Derek said. "Is it . . . disgusting? What does it even look like?"

Darkness's gaze shifted up. "You haven't looked at it?"

"No."

"Why?" Darkness asked.

He wasn't sure how to tell them, how the thought of looking in a mirror after the hallucinations this morning filled him with abject dread. Derek closed his eyes; it was too much to see their face and let the other voice speak at the same time.

"Scared."

To Derek, it still sounded like the voice inside his head, the interior monologue that narrated his thoughts and actions; flat, unresonant, a little hoarse, a little tired, used to an audience of only one. Nothing like the voice he employed on the sales floor, or with Tricia or his coworkers. Certainly not the one he had practiced in the mirror.

"It's not disgusting, Derek," Darkness said. "It's kinda hot, not gonna lie."

Derek kept his eyes shut. He didn't want to see if they were lying or telling the truth; both seemed equally devastating. Darkness was touching him so gently, like their fingers would soothe all the hurts on his body: the bruises and lacerations on his legs, the burns on his arms, the claw marks in his wrists. They ran their thumb just under the swell of his Adam's apple, brushing the lip of his defect. Derek felt it like an electric shock.

"You don't mean that," he said. Why did he feel like he was out of breath?

"I'm being one hundred percent sincere right now. It's weird and it's freaky, and maybe you didn't notice, but I'm kinda into that," they said quietly, like speaking at a normal volume might scare him off. Like he wasn't pinned down by the cool pressure of their fingers against the tenderest part of his throat. "But I'd rather die than let Dirk literally catch us with our pants down."

"That's a good point," he murmured, trying to pull himself out of the gravity of *but wait, I want to—*

Darkness must have noticed his struggle, and moved their hand off his neck, rubbing down Derek's shoulders and arms in a comforting, affectionate way. Unfortunately, they brushed right over where Dirk had shot him.

"What's—" Darkness said, then cut themself off when they saw the dark stain on the fabric. "Are you bleeding?"

Derek swallowed. "I guess so. Dirk shot a defekta that had wrapped itself around my arm."

Darkness helped him out of the coveralls. "Shit," they said. "This looks like a burn. That's from the INVENTERA?"

"An indirect shot," Derek explained, wincing as Darkness cleaned the wound. It was ugly, a series of wide, irregular burns, weeping clear fluid. His whole arm throbbed. "If you needed confirmation that I am defective, I guess that's it."

Derek hissed as Darkness pressed a compress against the worst of the burns, but it cooled his skin, and Derek sighed in relief as the prickling, throbbing ache abated.

"Fucking Dirk," they swore, and Derek was surprised to realize their hands were shaking. "The team used to be just the three of us, you know. Capturing and studying the defekta, not killing them. It was still shit work, and most INVENTERA teams walked off the job. When Dex ran away, they brought Dirk in to keep us in line. He's always been a piece of shit. We all knew it was just a matter of time before he did something really fucked up. We didn't want you to get stuck alone with him, but . . ."

"But I wanted to." Derek's knee-jerk admiration for Dirk was a bitter memory.

"Yeah," Darkness sighed. "And no offense, but I wasn't going to stick my neck out to keep you from crawling up his ass."

"He was just doing his job," Derek said after a long, shameful moment. "And doing it well. I thought that made us the most alike."

Darkness glared at him.

"I'm not excusing him," Derek explained. "This is literally his job. Exterminating the defekta. He's trying to distinguish himself at it."

"It's not just his job," Darkness said. They pulled the compress away and smoothed a sterile dressing over the burn. "Dirk takes pleasure in cruelty."

"But it doesn't matter if it's painless or cruel," Derek insisted. "It's still his job. Our job. He's just the most competent at it, so they put him in charge."

Darkness taped the dressing down, then sat back on their heels. "What were you planning when you came down here?"

"Oh, damn!" Derek hissed. He'd utterly forgotten his part of the plan. He stood up and zipped up his coveralls. "Where are the rest of the inventory team?"

"Dirk is still trying to track you down. Delilah and Dex are running interference and covering for me. He's going to get suspicious real soon, so we need to make some kind of plan."

"Way ahead of you," Derek said, making his way toward the wall by the cargo doors, where the automatic opener was bolted to the wall. "I'm running away."

"What?" Darkness hissed. "Derek—"

"I know, okay?"

"No, Derek—"

Derek steamrolled over their objections. "I've never worked anywhere else. I don't remember if I've ever *been* anywhere else. My memories don't go back further than November first, and I'm completely terrified of what I'm going to find out there. But I don't care. This is the best chance we have of surviving the night, and anything past that is a problem for Future Derek."

"You don't understand—wait, *we*?"

As if they'd been waiting for their cue, the cargo elevator doors opened, and the sofa and the SVINLÅDA, catching a ride on its cushions, made their slow way out through the aisles of stock and into the assembly area. The SVINLÅDA caught sight of Darkness and frantically clacked at the sofa to stop.

"This is the *we*, Derek?" Darkness said. "You're gonna run away with the defekta?"

The sofa and SVINLÅDA both looked at Derek, as if for translation. "They're okay," he said reassuringly. "They're on our side, I think."

When he turned to look back at Darkness, though, he saw

them staring at him, dumbfounded. "Do they understand you?" Darkness said.

"Yes?" he said.

Their voice rose a little higher. "Do you understand *them*?"

The sofa rumbled inquisitively at Derek, wanting to know if Darkness had become a threat. The SVINLÅDA clacked its support for the question.

"I guess I do," he said.

"You can communicate with them," Darkness said. "You can *translate* between us with your—" They flapped their hand at his neck. "Delilah is gonna flip her shit, she's been arguing for *months* with Resource Management—"

Derek was shaking his head rapidly. "No, no! I can't go to Resource Management! Dirk already tried to kill me, we're getting out of here."

He slapped the big green button on the side of the wall, and the door began its familiar, rattling ascent.

"Wait!" Darkness called.

The door rattled to a grinding stop. Derek hit the STOP button himself, not wanting to blow out the motor. He looked at the door and spotted a bright, shiny padlock attached to the door, latching it closed.

"We're locked in," Darkness said. "All the doors are padlocked. Even the emergency exits."

"Why would they do that?" Derek's mind was awash in OSHA violations.

Darkness shut their eyes, "I told you, INVENTERA teams had a habit of walking off the job. Dex ran away a couple months ago, and once they found him and dragged him back, there were a bunch of changes. Dirk took over as shift lead from Delilah, we get locked into the stores, and there are, uh.

Consequences planned, if we don't meet quotas."

"What kind of . . ." Derek started to ask, when he picked up the sound of footsteps rattling on the deathtrap spiral staircase. He grabbed Darkness and pulled them quickly back into the dark aisles of boxes and half-assembled furniture. Both the SVINLÅDA and sofa followed him—or attempted to, in the case of the sofa. It was too wide to fit into the aisles, so it settled down behind a couple pallets. Derek could feel it nervously trying to look like it belonged there; despite being a piece of furniture, it still failed to look casual.

"Can you get to the freight elevator if I distract Dirk?" Darkness whispered. "Take the defekta with you?"

"I guess?" he said doubtfully. It felt like he'd been running all night, doing nothing but trying to hide and evade and bluff and, inevitably, run away again. Now running meant leaving Darkness alone with Dirk.

"Good. Be careful." They pinched his cheek fondly. "Wouldn't want anything to happen to this pretty face."

They pushed him further into the aisle and then walked out into the muted light. "Hey," they said to Dirk. They were much better at acting casual than the sofa. Derek focused on sneaking out the other side of the aisle as quietly as he could, holding the SVINLÅDA so its footsteps wouldn't alert Dirk to their presence.

The sofa, poor thing, was trembling slightly when Derek snuck up behind it, gesturing for it to come away with him, back toward the freight elevator on the other side of the room.

He stopped a moment to listen to Dirk and Darkness, trying to gauge whether Dirk was sufficiently distracted for them to move.

"—supposed to *tell me* before you leave your post. Do you

do this just to annoy me? I know you're not as stupid as you look," Dirk said.

"That's one hell of a self-own," said Darkness, "considering we're *the same person*."

"Maybe, but I'm dressed to regulation, and you're dressed like a goddam freakshow."

"I'd rather be a freak than Reagan's pet bootlicker."

Derek could read the subtle signs of rage in Dirk's silence; the creak of his boots as he stepped closer to Darkness's space, the hiss of breath. All his attention was on Darkness now.

"You think dressing like this makes you better than us?" Dirk laughed. "So that we all know how different and special you are?"

Darkness yawned, loud and fake. "Yes, yes, how dare I attempt to assert my autonomy in the limited ways I'm allowed, truly shocking."

"It's the opposite of shocking," he sneered. "It's pathetic. All of you are pathetic, with your little pointless rebellions. You think the way you dress matters? You think changing your name to a random noun will accomplish anything?"

How had he ever thought that Dirk was a leader instead of a bully? He knew Darkness was doing this on purpose, holding out every red flag they could so Dirk would charge at them instead of him. He couldn't hurt them the way he could hurt Derek.

That didn't make Derek feel less awful about sneaking away. His attention was split between the escalating voices behind him, keeping the sofa next to him calm, and trying to keep his own noisy thoughts from broadcasting out to Dirk. Darkness knew what they were doing, he reminded himself. Darkness was doing this to protect him, and even if he was uncomfortable with that, it didn't mean—

"It accomplished pissing you off, and that honestly would have been enough. Maybe I should send Reagan a little note, let her know about this hostile work environment?"

Dirk hopefully didn't realize it, but the slick veneer of sarcasm coating Darkness's words masked a strain of very real anxiety. Derek could hear it in the way their voice tightened around the words, so different from when they were speaking a few minutes ago. They were holding their body so still, except for their hands, which were clenching compulsively into fists behind their back, squeezing so hard that Derek could nearly hear their bones creak.

Derek had told Reagan that he would sacrifice himself if there were no other choice. He'd elect to drown if there was no other way to save everyone else in the boat. How would Darkness have answered that question? Had they all been designed to answer that way, all of the D-64598s? To choose their own destruction over anything that could, so to speak, rock the boat?

Darkness had told him to go. Told him that they would distract Dirk so Derek could get away.

"And what do you think that will do?" Dirk said. "You know what happened the last time you reported me."

"That wasn't a report. I just relayed some concerns about your communications style to Reagan," said Darkness.

"Which she took very seriously, and then told us to handle internally. Isn't it great how hands-off they are?" Dirk asked cheerfully. "I hate being micromanaged."

"Yeah, I'd hate for any of us to experience actual consequences for how we treat each other. Wonder what would happen if one of us didn't come back? Think they'd still be super hands-off?"

They both laughed the same ugly, jagged laugh.

At some point, Derek had stopped moving. He and the couch stood stock-still, hidden by the pallets and tall aisles full of boxes. Dirk and Darkness weren't speaking now, and they weren't moving. Derek concentrated, but even his amplified senses couldn't pick out their separate heartbeats or inhalations from the ambient noise of the room. They just seemed to be standing, staring each other down. Derek covered his mouth, trying to dampen the sound of his own breathing.

"Where's your INVENTERA?" Dirk said suddenly.

Darkness didn't speak, and Derek felt his skin prickle with sudden panic.

"*Where is it?*" Dirk's voice like a whipcrack, shattering the quiet.

"Must have dropped it somewhere," Darkness said, their casual tone too thin to mask the fear in their voice. "Who the fuck cares, I can—"

Derek heard the dull impact on Darkness's flesh before their sharp cry.

"Where is he?" Dirk shouted. Derek, hating himself, hunkered down behind the couch, which rumbled warningly at him. He was digging his fingers into its upholstery now, nails biting into the fabric.

"Derek!" Dirk screamed into the room. "Derek, I know you're—"

There was a crash, a body hitting cement. Derek was off like he'd heard a starter's gun, leaping over the sofa with a hasty apology. Out of hiding, he could see Darkness and Dirk scuffling on the assembly room's floor. Darkness had knocked him down, but Dirk had quickly gotten the upper hand, pinning them and bringing his fist down onto their face, landing it solidly against their jaw.

Derek's vision wavered. He saw the destroyed table, the bloody embroidered cats on the table runner. All Dirk did was hurt things, and all Derek had done was stand by and let them get hurt.

Darkness's arm fell; they'd been knocked senseless. Dirk raised his fist again. Derek grabbed one of the long, silver torque wrenches off the assembly table. He aimed for his head, but Dirk twisted at the last second, looking back. The wrench hit him at the juncture of his shoulder and neck instead. It was enough to send him sprawling, and Derek reeled in a sympathetic shockwave from the impact. Dirk had talked about Derek's empathy as if it were a weakness; maybe it was if he couldn't even stand to see *Dirk* get hurt.

It didn't matter. Derek grabbed Darkness and hauled them up. He started toward the stairs again, but Darkness slurred, "Wait, wait," slipping out from under his arm.

They stumbled back over to where Dirk lay sprawled out on the floor, reared back, and kicked him in the face. Something crunched wetly, loud and resounding, and Derek gagged. Darkness steadied themself, pulling back for another kick, and Derek had to hiss out, "Don't! Please, don't, it's—"

Darkness looked at him, must have seen enough to understand: if they hit him again, Derek would probably drop as well. His guts were churning, and the wet snap of cartilage and bone was still echoing in his ears.

Darkness leaned over and spat on Dirk instead, with a muttered but heartfelt "Asshole."

Then they fumbled the INVENTERA out of the holster on Dirk's thigh and let Derek lead them away, hurrying them up the stairs.

Are your wormholes spawning syndicalists?

Members of the LitenVärld family learn early on about both the dangers and opportunities presented by maskhåls—wormholes that periodically open up in our stores, thanks to the unique quirk endemic in our layout and design. All managers, supervisors, and senior employees are trained in how to handle maskhåls. But there's another danger associated with this phenomenon:

Radicalizing our employees.

We have become aware that there are several adjacent universes with stores bearing the LitenVärld name but not our ethos. These stores have been infiltrated instead by radical agitators, who have, in some cases, violently taken over these stores with false promises of a worker utopia.

If your store experiences a maskhål, we recommend taking the following actions to protect your workers from this sort of dangerous propaganda:

- *Do not let your employees go through a maskhål without a FINNA, our patented navigational technology that will guide your employees only through approved alternative LitenVärlds.*
- *Reward your employees who successfully return. Gift cards, time off to recover, earlier shift picks for the following week. Do not give them obvious preferential treatment, though; this will breed resentment.*
- *If you must send a worker through a maskhål, remember to*

choose them in order of reverse seniority. If workers with little seniority are radicalized, it will be much easier to counteract this messaging.

If you are part of our D-64598 program, these workers have proven especially adept at resisting this kind of messaging from outside agitators, and are deeply loyal to the LitenVärld family. We recommend adding them to any team to counteract any outside agitation.

And above all: remain vigilant! Make sure that your wormholes aren't exposing your workers to the dangers of subversive and radical beliefs.

Memo sent to LitenVarld managers and supervisors

Chapter 8

Changing the World,
One Room at a Time!

At the top of the stairs, the fuzzy panic in Derek's head started to clear. They needed to get somewhere safe, and they needed to hide. They couldn't do either alone.

"Hide us?" he shakily whispered to the defekta around him. He could sense them so much better now, the tiny movements that gave them away: the breaths they held, the weight of their attention. They weren't overtly friendly like the SVINLÅDA or helpful and comforting like the sleeper sofa. They'd heard Derek's pleas earlier, done the smart thing and hidden, sometimes in plain sight. They were all sizes, all shapes; flat modular walls, hefty floor lamps, and tiny strings of bulbs. A rosy purple chaise longue regarded him warily, while a fake ficus plant waved at him in agitation. These defekta's first concern was their own survival; Derek couldn't fault them for it.

"We just need time to figure out a plan," he begged.

Derek could hear the stairs rattling behind them.

"Please." The word dragged out of him, sharp-edged and catching on his throat and tongue. Darkness squeezed his arm.

In front of him, a full-sized corner KLÄDHÅL wardrobe blinked its eyes open at them, then slid open its doors. As Derek ducked into it, he noted that it was much sturdier than when he had assembled it, the plastic structure now like bone, and that the plywood backing had transformed into thick and leathery folds of skin, sparsely furred where he pushed through them, exiting out the other side.

He helped Darkness out through the narrow slit—trying not to think too hard about what purpose that orifice served. A modular wall rolled forward, propelled by a handful of decorative wooden STAVA letters, and Derek and Darkness slipped into a showroom on a totally different track of the store. Even if Dirk still had the map with all of Derek's shortcuts, even if he ran at full speed, they'd bought themselves a few precious minutes. The STAVA letters slipped the wall back, smoothly working as a team to bolt it into place.

He gave Darkness a quick once-over, trying to remember what they'd done while examining him for a concussion. Their jaw and cheek were swelling and discolored, mottled red and purple, but their eyes were shining happily.

"I broke his nose. I broke Dirk's fucking nose." They grinned triumphantly, uncaring or maybe not noticing the blood pinking their teeth.

Derek suppressed the shudder that tried to work its way up his shoulders as he remembered the wet snap of cartilage. "I saw. You're lucky he didn't do the same to you, or worse."

"It's not luck when a friend saves you from getting the shit beat out of you," They gingerly touched the bruises blooming on their face. "This is definitely the best *and* worst shift I've ever had."

"Me too," he said.

"I fucking *knew* the rooms were changing around on me. Sorry, I'm just feeling very vindicated right now. In the grand scheme of things, we're probably fucked, but I was right *and* I got to fuck up Dirk's face."

"We can celebrate when we're out of here," Derek said, though he had no idea how they would do that. The doors were still locked, Dirk was still chasing them. They still had nowhere to go.

"We need to get back to Dex and Delilah," Darkness said. "I'm not going anywhere without them."

"Can we trust them?"

Darkness stared at him, turning their head to see him better out of their unswollen eye. "Of course you can trust them."

"There's no *of course*," he reminded them. "Why would they go against the company just to save a bunch of defekta?"

Derek's pulse was picking up again, banging against his ribs, blood pounding in his throat. Why couldn't this be simple? Why couldn't they just get from point A to point B?

Darkness had unmuted their earpiece and chimed the other two members of the inventory team. "Guys, where are you?"

"Customer service desk," Dex answered. "Got you two on the shoplifting cameras, but not Delilah."

"Bathrooms, I think?" Delilah answered. "By the new VIP lounge. I can hear that damn toilet lurking. Where are *you*? Are you okay? What happened?"

"We don't have time to explain," Derek said, too anxious to let Darkness launch into the full story. "Dirk is—he's—"

"Is he dead?" asked Dex. "Is it too much to hope that the toilet ate him?"

"Now there's a thought," Delilah mused. "Maybe we can let them loose on each other."

"*No*," Derek hissed. He wasn't going to let Dirk near any of the defekta, not even the egg chair toilet. "He's *our* problem. We have to deal with him."

"You don't think we've tried?" Delilah said. "We've been dealing with him for *months*. Try to even imagine what that's like, Derek."

Derek did imagine it; all the careful ways that the other three watched out for each other, bit back their words and didn't argue when Dirk lashed out, but kept each other's spirits up. He'd known that they were broken somehow but hadn't understood what broke them. But maybe his urge to be the solution was correct; he just couldn't do that alone.

"Stay where you are," he told Dex and Delilah. "We'll make our way over to you."

He muted his earpiece again, then held his breath to listen. Dirk was getting closer, but he'd need to get all the way to the front of the store before he could turn back toward them. Derek could hear dozens of defekta in between those two points. The disorientation is by design, Dirk had said. What if they took over the design? Made the disorientation work for them?

"This is our store," he whispered to them.

He could feel the defekta's attention, their curiosity. They'd heard the promise of death in Dirk's footfalls through the store. They'd heard the pain he caused to the defekta, to Derek, and now to Darkness.

Hiding wasn't a solution. It didn't even resolve their fear; the longer you hid, the more afraid you felt, the larger the possibility of getting caught loomed, more inevitable with each near escape.

But the defekta had lived day and night in the labyrinth. They *were* the labyrinth, designed to ensnare unwary customers with diversions and digressions, pulling them off their intended paths.

"We know it better than he does," Derek said. He was finally able to speak in both his voices and say the same thing to speak with purpose and mean it with his whole heart. And the defekta heard him; they were hanging on the harmony of every word.

"Help him get lost," he said. Then, because it was polite, he added, "Please."

All around them, the store came alive. Not just between them and Dirk, but in all sections, even the ones they'd scanned and cleared, defekta seemed to shake themselves awake and begin to move.

(Was that how the defekta spread? One voice entreating others to wake, so the silence wasn't so toxically lonely?)

The labyrinth of showrooms started twisting and changing in a strange, collective choreography, furniture shifting and snaking past the rearranging walls. If the shifting colors of a kaleidoscope could be translated into sound, Derek thought, that's what it was like.

When the store was busy, there was a hum of sorts, almost a song that threaded through the blanketing noise of a hundred small sounds. Even before Derek had started changing, before he became *defective*, he heard it. Derek would find himself stopping during his shift to listen to the store, marveling at its layers and complexity. And like nearly everything did, it had reminded him that he was alone, a point of silence and stillness at the heart of it.

But now he knew that he was inextricable from the tapestry of sound, the living and chaotic symphony. Now that same hum of activity filled the store. It wasn't the same without the dozens of customers wandering through the showrooms, cranky and lost and entitled. It was *better*, more focused; a chorus of voices instead of an unrehearsed mob of disparate notes.

"Holy shit," he heard Dex say in his earpiece. "Uh, guys? Is this normal?"

Derek could feel the rest of the inventory team as points of stillness, with the defekta orbiting around them warily without getting too close.

"No, definitely not normal, but it's not like normal was any good," Delilah said, though she still sounded alarmed. "Are we in danger?"

"It's okay," Darkness assured them. "Just sit tight. We'll come to you."

"Awesome," said Dex. He sounded enthused for the first time since Derek had met him. "This is so cool."

"Dex? Dex!" Delilah said. "Do *not* put this on SnapYap."

"Too late, I'm definitely putting this on SnapYap. This is like, content gold."

Delilah sighed. "Forget it, I'm—"

Delilah fell silent as, through her earpiece, the rest of them heard a warped version of "Clair de Lune."

"I think the egg chair toilet decided to join the party," she whispered.

Derek pulled his earpiece out and shut his eyes, trying to pinpoint the toilet. It was close to her, closer than Delilah probably realized. It wasn't moving toward her, though, not breaching the diameter of stillness the defekta had left around her. Derek couldn't be sure, but it seemed to be listening. Observing, the same way that Derek had.

He'd unpack that later, when there wasn't a homicidal supervisor running around.

"Can you help us?" he asked the defekta. He was reasonably sure he could navigate the maze himself, but didn't want to risk running into Dirk. "We need to go to the center of the store."

Down by their feet, a fake plant—standing on its fronds like they were spider's legs—waved its ceramic base, gesturing for them to follow it through the ever-shifting labyrinth. Before they could reach the others, Derek was distracted by a strange hum, a dissonant note amid the harmonies—like the same melody played in a different key.

"You don't hear that, do you?" he asked, pausing in a space that looked like an art deco drawing room had collided with a cottagecore kitchen. "It's like—I can't describe it, but it's weird. Out of place."

"The furniture is alive and dancing, Derek," said Darkness. "This is all weird."

Derek was still trying to find words to describe the exact definitions of this *particular* weirdness when Darkness gave a punched-out huff of surprise.

"What is it?"

Darkness pointed at a white bathroom vanity, reaching a stubby marble leg forward to prod at a wall that was stretching and sagging, like some unseen force was pressing it out of shape. It looked threadbare somehow; Derek could just barely make out the shapes of things moving on the other side of it.

He still didn't understand until Darkness said, "Maskhål. Or the beginnings of one, maybe."

Of course. And it wasn't the only one: Derek could hear thin spots singing all over the store, with wavering pitches that rose and fell to their own alien cadences, all of them distinct from each other and from the intimately familiar song of *his* store. The tangled layout of LitenVärld's sales floor already put a lot of stress on reality; the rooms and paths moving on their own must be stretching it to the breaking point.

"Nobody wander off, okay?" Darkness said into the comms. "The maze just got a lot bigger."

• • •

At the customer service desk, Dex had his head bent over his phone, not even watching the monitors, which was possibly why he didn't notice their approach until they were a few feet away. He flinched, bringing up his INVENTERA halfway to a shooting position before catching sight of Darkness. Derek's nerves, soothed by walking through the store as defekta danced joyfully past them, started jangling again.

"Dex!" Darkness hissed. They punched him in the arm. "Someday you're going to walk into traffic with your nose stuck in that thing, and none of us are going to stop you."

"Fine, that's fair, but *look*!" He waved his phone at them. "It's been like three minutes and my post is blowing up. I've gotten two hundred reposts on two different platforms and forty new followers."

Sensing minimal interest from Darkness, Dex turned on Derek, shoving his phone entreatingly at him. Derek played the video, which was only seventeen seconds long. It started with blurry CCTV footage of the sales floor breaking into choreographed movement, like one of the old Elvis films that played on a loop in the Rockabilly Hideaway suite. Then it panned up, to show the area right in front of the customer service desk. It was a wider panorama than you got in most of the store, where the twisting walkways between rooms only let you see a narrow few feet ahead. From behind the customer service desk, though, Dex had been able to record a few seconds of dozens of defekta moving together in a coordinated dance, then set it to an incongruously perky pop song.

Dex took his phone back, scrolled down, and laughed breathlessly. "Holy shit, three hundred reposts."

"If you're able to tear yourselves away from social media for a second," Delilah whispered tensely, "I'm kind of pinned down here."

"Shit, right," Dex said, shoving his phone back in his pocket. He picked up the INVENTERA from where he'd left it on the counter and, showing significantly more sensitivity than Derek would have thought him capable of, noticed that Derek flinched. "Uh, you okay?" Then, catching sight of the bruises on Darkness's jaw, "Wait, what the fuck happened to your *face?*"

"Dirk," Darkness answered simply.

" . . . I'll fucking kill him," Dex said mutinously.

"You'll have to get in line," Delilah said, apparently listening to their conversation.

"Maybe it can be a group effort. Our first real team-bonding exercise." Darkness reached over and plucked the INVENTERA from Dex's unresisting grip. "Also, new policy: ditch the INVENTERAS."

"Why are we ditching the only weapons we have against the defekta?" Delilah asked.

They dumped Dex's gun and the one they'd taken off Dirk into the trashcan beneath the counter. "We don't need them. Derek?"

Derek looked for the FALSKA artificial plant that had led him and Darkness here. It had hung back from Dex and the customer service desk, but came over when Derek called it. "Would you mind helping us get to the VIP lounge?" he asked.

Dex wheeled back a couple steps as the FALSKA approached, but Darkness grabbed him by the wrist. "It's fine, don't be a baby about it," they said.

"Hey, fuck you, I'm not a baby," he spat. But he was still obviously nervous, allowing Darkness to pull him along by the wrist as they followed the FALSKA.

"So, is he like the defekta whisperer," Dex said to Darkness in what he probably assumed was an undertone.

"It's not really whispering," Darkness answered. "It's just talking."

"And listening," Derek said. "That's the important bit."

. . .

The VIP lounge was in a slightly sunken part of the sales floor—unconsciously urging customers down toward it while making it more difficult to leave. The flood that Derek had encountered early in the night had pooled in the lowest part of the sales floor, surrounding the VIP lounge with a moat. The emergency lights beneath it wavered, throwing up shifting reflections onto its walls.

The defekta surrounding the VIP lounge had quickly adapted to the aquatic environment. Derek stepped gingerly into the water, not out of distaste for the cold water flooding his boots, but because he was distracted by a school of small fish darting around his feet, cutting through the water with a silvery glint. One seemed to pause before him, investigating his waterlogged boots. Beneath the murky water, Derek made out the smooth bowl and gilt handle of a soup spoon, which had sprouted tiny, transparent fins. It darted away with the rest of the school of flatware when Derek took another step.

The adaptations were startling. Elsewhere in the store, the

defekta were either quick and mobile, evolving lanky limbs capable of darting through the shadows, or large and slow, but normal-looking. Long, tuberous shoots had sprouted from an ornately carved chaise longue, and its velvet cushions were covered with a Technicolor array of tiny, blooming flowers. Creatures floated through the water: sets of prestige water glasses and tumblers propelling themselves like jellyfish, an umbrella stand with a Lichtenstein print that Derek knew cost over a thousand dollars undulating through the mud.

Dex had his phone out again, training the camera on a series of plants floating on the surface of the water, bright green with deep purple veins and wide-mouthed yellow flowers. They bore a startling resemblance to one of the throw pillow designs. Some of the smaller electric NUMINÖS candles crouched atop them like toads, letting out small, reedy sounds.

"Del?" Darkness whispered. "Where are you?"

"Crouched behind an armoire. Be careful, that toilet is fully stealthed, I haven't been able to get a bead on it."

"It's probably hiding because it doesn't want to get shot again," Derek said, annoyed.

Derek could hear the strains of Debussy, and the others soon picked it up as well: the distorted, dissonant version of "Clair de Lune," notes stretched and eerie.

At least to their ears. The toilet wasn't trying to scare them, Derek thought. It was only singing to keep itself company.

Derek thought back to their earlier encounter; it had come far out into the store, searching for something. Had it been lonely like Derek? Had it remembered him from the night before, when he'd been sick in it? That was embarrassing.

"Hi," he said to the toilet. The piano hit a sour note and cut out as it realized Derek was speaking to it, fading into a gut-

tural growl that radiated threat. The toilet was fully camouflaged, managing to hide in nothing but shadows. Derek could
hear the smaller defekta around him scatter for their own hiding places.

"Derek, what are you doing?" Delilah hissed.

"I'm sorry about what happened earlier," he said, ignoring
Delilah. "I couldn't understand you, and I was frightened. I'm
sorry you got hurt."

It was terrifying to speak so plainly; to give up all the quirks
of speech and body language that Derek had used to disguise
himself, make him seem smaller, less strange, less needy, less
like he was swallowing down a scream.

The toilet stopped growling at him and slowly sloughed
off its camouflage; cautiously rewarding Derek's vulnerability
with its own. Dex and Darkness both took a couple steps back
as the toilet slowly faded into sight. Derek could see the burn
where Dirk had shot it, charred black with cobalt-blue flesh
underneath it. It looked painful.

"Yeah, he hurt me, too." Derek rolled up his sleeves, showing off the bandages. The egg chair toilet took a couple steps
forward, cautious, ready to flee. "I should have stopped him,
but I was . . ."

It wasn't pain that made Derek's throat clench. It was shame,
and horror, and the overwhelming awfulness of seeing two defekta blown apart and being too afraid to stop it.

"Derek."

He turned around to see Delilah standing behind him; she
must have come out from behind the armoire while he was
talking to the toilet. He swiped angrily at his eyes; he didn't
deserve the comfort of crying. He'd gotten some burns on his
arm. Two defekta were dead, and the rest of the inventory

team had had to put up with Dirk for *months*. He'd only had a few hours of him.

"You can talk to them," she said. "And they understand you?"

"I think I'm one of them." Scraping up the last of his rapidly dwindling bravery, he rolled down his turtleneck, feeling the cool, damp air on his defect. "See?" he said, tense, waiting for the other shoe to drop, or for her to shoot him on the spot.

"Holy shit," Dex said from behind her. "That's fucking *gross*."

There was a thump as Darkness punched him in the shoulder.

"Hey, fuck you! I didn't mean it in a bad way!"

Delilah said nothing, just considered him with a look of genuine surprise on her face.

"I didn't realize what it was until, you know. Until Dirk tried to kill me."

But that wasn't entirely true; he'd known something was wrong with him. He knew enough to hide it, knew it would get him in trouble and endanger his relationship with LitenVärld; that LitenVärld, despite Derek's genuine love for it and his faith in its ethos, would not or could not make space for him to exist as his whole self. There was a place for everything here, but—as Darkness had pointed out early in the night—that was only true so long as LitenVärld could control it or sell it. Anything the company couldn't make use of, they disposed of. That's what they'd done with the discordant inventory team members. That's what they'd done with Derek when he stepped out of line and asked for a day off. And naturally, that's what they'd done with all the defekta.

Derek felt grief bearing down on him, clenching in his stomach. It hurt; this was the only home he had, and it had rejected him and wanted him dead. Worse, he hadn't cared that it did this to others until he'd experienced the pain himself.

"I don't know what to do," he said, both to the inventory team and the toilet, as well as the rest of the defekta—they'd all crept close, inveterate eavesdroppers that they were. "I can't stay with the company. I can't ask you to—"

"You can ask," Delilah said. "You should ask."

That robbed Derek of his words. He'd reached the end of his courage, and now felt terribly afraid. Not even that they would refuse him; if they said yes, it opened up a whole barrel of complications, and Derek wasn't sure if he was strong enough to deal with them.

Still. He forced the words out, because speaking didn't always require courage; sometimes desperation was enough.

"How do you feel about quitting?" Derek asked.

"Fan-fucking-tastic," said Darkness.

"Awesome," Dex agreed.

"Great," said Delilah. "But I think we can do a little better than just resigning."

• • •

"Does the company actually value Dirk the way he thinks they do?" Derek asked Delilah. They were sitting together in the customer service desk, lit a little better than the rest of the dim store. She had asked if she could record a few observations about his defect for her notes; she'd never given up on trying to understand the defekta, and her focus now extended to Derek's defect.

"I doubt it," Delilah said, looking critically at the anatomical sketch she'd made in a leatherbound notebook. Derek didn't quite dare to look at it himself, but couldn't make himself look totally away, so it lingered in his peripheral vision in graphite, surrounded by Delilah's dense, cramped handwriting. *Tympanal plate??? Auditory vesicles interpreting transmitting lies as pain—*

"He's discordant too, though he always liked to forget that fact. They put him in charge, and they definitely like him more than us, but that's one hell of a low bar."

"Still," Derek said. "There won't be any going back after this."

Delilah looked at him over the tops of the UPPFATTA reading glasses she'd perched on her nose. "Do you really think any of us want to go back?"

Derek opened his mouth, then hesitated.

"Do you?" Delilah added. "It's okay if you do want to."

"I can't, though," Derek said. "I mean, look at me."

Derek had finally given up on the turtleneck, torn and splattered with blood, and was pulling on a V-neck that he nervously stole from the FUNDAMENT collection of plain shirts, underpants, and pajamas. His defect was tucked into the hollow of his throat, not as large or terrible as it had felt, but he still couldn't look long at his reflection in any of the many mirrors throughout the store. He bore scratches on his wrists from the dying table runner, bruises and gashes all over his legs from his first encounter with the egg chair toilet, burns from the INVENTERA. Reagan had told him that he wasn't a normal employee, but an exceptional one, and that alone placed a different set of expectations on him. If only she could see him now.

Well. She probably *would* see him soon. Dex had plans for more videos, since the first one had gone viral. It was only a matter of time before it got back to LitenVärld corporate.

"It's okay to wish you could go back, even if you can't," Delilah said thoughtfully. "This has all happened really quickly for you. We've had months to come up with a million failed escape schemes."

"Like what?" Derek asked.

Delilah put down the field notebook, and Derek could finally look away. Nearby, Darkness and Dex were trying to teach a group of defekta the choreography of a dance that had gone viral on ChitChat. The egg chair toilet was both the most enthusiastic and the objectively worst dancer.

"Oh, all kinds of stuff. We alerted the media through anonymous tip-offs, but all the true things we told them sounded like pranks, and when we toned it down they told us that there wasn't enough interest to report or investigate. And it's really difficult to make a plan that would actually surprise your supervisor when he's basically the same person as you, can extrapolate all the ideas in our heads. Last time we just ran. Only Dex made it out, and he got dragged back after a week. That's when the company started locking us in." She tapped her notebook contemplatively. "You're the difference this time. And we've learned enough from all of our previous failures to know how to seize this chance and do something with it."

Derek mulled this over, wondering how many of the plans that they made were similar to the ones he'd tried to enact. "Is it weird to be grateful that you failed all those times? I mean, I'm directly benefiting from it now, and if you hadn't, I'd still be . . ."

Trapped, he thought. Treading water.

He flinched a little from a touch on his shoulder. Delilah had leaned forward and put her warm hand on his arm. "We're not doing this as a favor to you. This isn't a rescue mission for the defekta, or a noble sacrifice. We're all in this stupid boat to-gether."

Derek huffed half a laugh. At Delilah's raised eyebrow, he ex-plained, "Sorry, I was just thinking of a question Reagan asked me when she interviewed—or I guess interrogated—me ear-lier today."

"Oh, the question about the people in the sinking boat? She *loves* that question. I feel like that's the real LitenVärld ethos, right there. Anytime there's a problem, throw the least conve-nient people overboard."

Derek felt his urge to defend the company rise, sputter out, and disintegrate. That's what happened when you were the person elected to drown.

"Dirk's getting closer," he said, pitching his voice loud enough to get Darkness and Dex's attention. "I think it's time."

"Gotta say, this plan is weird," Dex said.

"None of our plans have worked," Delilah reminded them. "But it'll be another point of data."

Darkness nodded and added, "And it's got style. We'll make failing look cool, if nothing else."

The egg chair toilet, having followed Dex back to the group like a lost puppy, rippled with enthusiasm as it leaned its cold weight against Derek's leg. Once Derek had apologized and explained what had happened, the egg chair toilet had trans-formed into an enthusiastic ally, overjoyed to be part of a group, and possibly a little attention-starved. It reminded him of a puppy—a very large porcelain puppy that weighed a few hundred pounds and could completely camouflage itself.

"Do you want one of us to come with you? " Delilah asked.

Derek shook his head. He'd told them he didn't want to

risk one of them going in and getting lost, falling through a maskhål without any way of finding their way back. But also—and he hadn't told them this—he felt like Dirk was his responsibility; as the person who'd had the least exposure to him, as the person who'd refused to see how awful he was until it was too late. He couldn't look at Darkness's bruised face or the dark circles under Delilah's eyes or the way Dex always hunched in on himself when talking about the things he liked—he couldn't know where those things came from and ask any of them to do this in his place.

And Derek wasn't alone anyway. The defekta would have his back. There were always monsters in the hearts of mazes—there was definitely a picture book in the KinderVärld children's line with that title—but this maze was on Derek's side.

"I can do this," he said.

"We'll be watching on CCTV and listening over comms," Delilah reminded him. "And we can always go back to Plan B if this doesn't work."

Plan B was to murder Dirk. Derek had barely managed to convince everyone not to make it Plan A.

All Derek had to do now was to walk the labyrinth, slow enough for Dirk to follow him into a different world, and then lose him there.

Derek had spent this whole shift running away from things—now he would run toward something. That was some kind of progress.

"This will work," he said to the group, trying to scrape together some confidence. It had to work. He hated Dirk, despite not being built to hate. But his ears started ringing and his body broke out into a cold, prickly sweat when he imagined Plan B.

Delilah patted him on the back, and Dex offered him a fist bump, giving a pained sigh when Derek fumbled it in a moment of extreme squareness.

Darkness just slid into Derek's space before he could try to think of something to say to them. They pressed their warm body against him and touched their uninjured cheek to his. "I'd kiss you for luck if my face didn't hurt so fucking bad," they whispered.

Derek made a noise he had never made before. Darkness laughed, winked at him when they parted, and Derek flushed.

"Gross," Dex muttered.

Derek practically flung himself into the maze after that, with Darkness's laughter fading in his ears. He made his way to Dirk's footsteps, which were pounding against the cement in a rage that grew louder and louder the closer Derek got to him. Derek could make out muttered curses, just on the edge of hearing, promises of what he was going to do to the defekta, what he would get LitenVärld to do to Derek, to his whole traitorous team.

Around him, the defekta were still moving. Walls parted, curtains tugged themselves out of his way, shelves skipped aside, and couches shuffled over to let him past. He found himself opening a shower door and walking into it, then crawling through the resultant passageway as it heaved arrhythmic breaths around him. A napkin set whose cotton weave had solidified into leathery wings with tasteful geometric borders led him through the narrow passageways as they opened and closed around him.

He knew the exact moment when Dirk saw him. Derek had paused to catch his breath and his bearings, in what had at one point been Kitchens, but now had a little bit of every part of the store; a breakfast table had shimmied over to a secretary desk, while a set of bocce balls from Backyard and Recreation and some decorative floral wreaths rolled around his legs.

Dirk's steps slowed and then paused as some predatory instinct made him look Derek's way, separated only by a few rooms, and visible through a set of glass French doors.

Their eyes met, and Derek held his gaze. Dirk really did look like a monster haunting a maze. Blood had dried in streams down his face, while bruising had spread over his nose and up into his eyes and cheeks. Blood-flecked spittle had collected in the corners of his mouth. This was Dirk, the truth of him, beneath the confidence and self-assurance, beneath the easy authority and casual bullying. Derek was ashamed that he hadn't seen it before; even more ashamed that there were so few differences between them.

He darted away. Dirk thundered after him in pursuit.

Derek aimed himself toward one of the thinnest places, a spot that was already stretched nearly to the breaking point beneath the weight of LitenVärld's uncanny geometries. Its wailing became a whistling shriek as it split open, and Derek broke into a sprint. A bright blue shelving unit pried apart its shelves just enough for Derek to wriggle through. Beyond it, the maskhål stretched across a passageway, the same red as the emergency lights, throbbing as if to a heartbeat. Derek waited until he could hear Dirk only a dozen feet behind him, and then darted through.

This was the part that most worried Derek; that in the other world, the defekta wouldn't listen to him, or be able to understand him, or that they wouldn't be alive at all. Delilah had told him that the closest universes would almost undoubtedly be the most similar to theirs. The further out one ventured out, the stranger and more divergent the universes became.

The shifting labyrinth had extended past the borders of his own world. The defekta here were still moving, still remaking the maze as he ran through it.

"Thank you," he said as he passed them, because they owed him nothing but were saving his life anyway.

As he ran, Derek tried to balance his own pursuit with Dirk's, chasing after the sound of the maskhåls as they split open doorways into other doorways into doorways; he couldn't let himself get too far ahead, nor let Dirk get too close.

He was concentrating on that balance so much that he didn't hear the other footsteps in the maze, not until he collided with them.

"Sorry!" he said instinctively.

"Sorry!" the other voice said, in the exact same intonation, at the exact same time.

Seeing the other members of the inventory team for the first time had been like looking into a series of warped mirrors. This was like looking into a perfectly, painfully accurate one. Dex and Delilah and Darkness might share his genetic material, but they were thoroughly their own people.

This was *Derek*, down to his bones, down to the scuffs on his work boots and pinched line between his eyebrows.

"You're . . ." the other one said, pointing at him. He had the same look of shock that Derek could feel spreading on his own features. "I guess I should stop being surprised at this point."

"Maybe," Derek confirmed. He pointed behind him. "You came in here to lose Dirk?"

"Uh-huh," the other Derek said, jerking his head backward in confirmation. "Think we should—"

"Together?" Derek said. "Oh, absolutely."

They both took off, twin footfalls thudding down the hall-ways as they shifted around them.

"What if they see each other?" other Derek asked, out of breath. "The Dirks, I mean?"

Derek looked at him. "What *if* they see each other?"

He and the other Derek ran in silence for a moment, thoughts racing.

"I am *so* tired of being chased."

"Same. They might distract each other."

"At least enough for us to sneak away and leave them here."

"I can't think of a worse punishment for Dirk than having to deal with himself."

"Exactly."

It didn't take long for the two Dirks' footsteps to collide, much the way that Derek's and the other Derek's had. Their crash was much louder and harder, both of them cursing aloud. Derek and alt-Derek slowed down, then paused to listen.

"What—?" Dirk screamed. "Who the hell are you?"

"Who the hell are *you*?"

Neither of them answered, but they weren't stupid, and it didn't take long before one of them guessed what had happened.

"He led you through a wormhole," one of them said. "I can't believe you fell for that."

"Hey, how do you know *you* didn't go through a wormhole? Fucking prick. No wonder everyone hates you."

"Hey, fuck *you*, buddy. Attitudes like that are why you haven't gotten ahead."

"Fuck me? Fuck *you*!"

Derek had thought Dirk had been joking when he'd said

that seeing his doppelgängers had made him feel violent rage. Maybe he'd meant Derek to think it was a joke, but the situation wasn't funny now. He and the other Derek both winced as they felt a fist connect with someone's body. He jerked his head in the opposite direction. "Should we get out of here?"

The other Derek nodded, and they quietly made their way further into the endless labyrinth, the sound of the two Dirks scrapping and screaming slowly fading away.

• • •

For a while they walked aimlessly in silence. The defekta seemed to have finally tired themselves out, and the labyrinth stopped shifting and moving around them.

"I think I need a break," Derek said.

"Same," the other Derek said, and they smiled exhaustedly at each other.

They stopped in one of the newly chaotic rooms; a dining room table was crowded in next to a child's pink-and-purple canopy bed, with a glass-top coffee table at its foot. The coffee table rippled a half-hearted welcome to them. Derek collapsed onto the bed, which shuffled grumpily under him, while alt-Derek slid down the wall, leaning heavily on the table.

Derek glanced over at his otherworldly counterpart, and found his gaze drawn to his defect.

It was a delicate-looking thing, a narrow pink slash like a lipless mouth that stretched across his Adam's apple. It gaped a little bit, just enough for Derek to get a glimpse of intricate folds of skin inside, tiny and nearly invisible hairs dotted along the flesh.

"It's not as bad as I thought it would be," alt-Derek said.

Derek looked up to see that he was being stared at with the same scrutiny. He swallowed nervously.

"Sorry! I didn't mean to stare."

"It's fine, of course," said alt-Derek. "I hadn't really gotten up the courage to look at my own, but yours was . . ."

"Oh, me neither," Derek laughed. "And I don't know if they're the same, yours is really pretty small. Definitely not as bad as—"

"Yours too," said alt-Derek. "I think I really blew it out of proportion in my mind."

"It's easier, isn't it?" Derek said. "To confront the things that scare you when it's, you know. Not you."

The silence spun out between them for a long moment, until Derek asked, "What are you going to do now?"

The other Derek didn't answer for a moment, then sighed, "It's a good question."

"Do you not want to answer it?" Derek asked.

"I'm just saying—it's really nice to be able to ask that question. It's a good question to have."

Derek smiled after a moment and nodded in agreement. He wasn't sure if the other Derek meant that it was nice to be able to sit and plan something out, or that it was so rare that they'd had *options*. Either way, Derek let himself wallow in the luxury of choice for a few moments, lying back and staring up at the gauzy pink canopy of the bed, which had little firefly-shaped lights embedded in it that pulsed in rhythmic bursts of light.

After a while, he knew it was time to go. He wanted to go back to the rest of the inventory team, to his store and the defekta that had remade it. He felt a moment of panic as he searched for the sound of *his world,* its distinct pitch and rhythm—what if he couldn't find it? what if the maskhål had collapsed and he was stuck?—until he found it again, ringing clear in the distance. He was part of the labyrinth, just like the other defekta, and knew how to shape it.

"I think I'm going to head back."

"Yeah, it's about time, huh?"

They both stood, considering each other for a moment.

And because it was so much easier to say it to somebody else, he told the other Derek, "You deserve better than what LitenVärld was willing to give you."

The other Derek hunched in embarrassment for a moment, then straightened up and said, "You're worth more than what you can do for other people."

Derek grimaced a little, feeling the words settle heavily on him.

"Good luck," he said to Derek, and to himself. "For whatever comes next."

They shook hands and turned back toward their respective worlds.

Email sent to: ResDevVP@LitenVärld.univ, ResourceMgVP@LitenVärld.univ

CC: BOD@LitenVärld.univ

From: ReaganKoch@LitenVärld.univ

SUBJ: Re:Re:Re:Re:[IMMEDIATE RESPONSE REQUIRED: Situation at Store 7748]

All,

Please find the forwarded list of demands below. I am well aware that this is unprecedented and outside of our normal playbook, so let's all keep cool heads. My read on this situation is as follows, in bullet point format because I've been awake since 3AM with the store manager, whose sobriety is definitely suspect.

- All attempts to contact the team's leader (D-64598-01-6-13-150, designation "Dirk") have been met with no answer, though this does not confirm or deny any claims about his death or defection to another universe.

- We're able to access CCTV, but it only uploads to the cloud every six hours, so it doesn't help us get an accurate view of events right now. We're working on ways to access the store's internal network remotely. At the moment, we only have the team's word and the video footage that they've sent us to go on.

- If their video footage is to be trusted (and we're reasonably certain that they do not have access to any software that could be used to doctor it), this is one of the largest and most serious outbreaks of defekta that we've seen.

- The store is effectively held hostage. There is enough food in the food court that starving them out would not be easy, even if we cut the electricity and they lost all perishables. Cutting the heat might freeze them out, but given the current temperatures, we would likely end up dealing with numerous burst pipes, with the potential to lose the entire inventory—a loss that could be too great for this store to recover from, given its underperformance at Christmas.

- Obviously some of these demands are non-starters, and others are simply jokes. I'm familiar enough with the team in question to recognize their attempts at humor. Unfortunately, like I said, the store is effectively held hostage, and we have a short timeline before customers start arriving. The store manager assured me that they have the normal set of elderly customers that always show up at opening to get their step-count in and take advantage of the food court's Early Bird special.

- If the team has actually managed to ally with the defekta inside—and again, we have no reason to believe that their video footage is anything but real—this has extremely troubling implications for future extermination efforts, which have had middling success so far.

- We are less than a week away from the grand opening of the VIP program, which has been a costly investment. LitenVärld does not need the scrutiny that a full siege or frontal assault on the store would bring, counter to some of the suggestions that have been made in this thread.

- Please re-familiarize yourselves with the definition of the <u>sunk cost fallacy</u> and <u>Einstein's definition of insanity</u> before responding.

- I don't believe in negotiating with terrorists either, Jerome, but some of these demands offer far more elegant solutions than anyone in R&D has been able to come up with after four months, an army of unpaid interns, and a wildly bloated budget. *Glass freaking houses, Jerome.*

Please review the demands below before our conference call at 05:30 CST and be ready to make some pragmatic choices.

QUOTED TEXT:

to whom it may concern:

This is Delilah, Darkness, and Dex, remaining members of the short-lived INVENTERA division, and Derek, our newest comrade. Dirk is permanently indisposed. ¯_(ツ)_/¯

To replace our lost leader, we have made allies with the defekta. We have set aside our mutually assured destruction in favor of screwing up your week, which is a much more laudable goal. We would like to open negotiations about the collective working conditions for discordant and defekt LitenVärld models. We will remain locked in the store until the following demands are met, or a collective agreement is reached.

Here is our opening list of demands:

1) A 24-pack of beer, delivered immediately

2) 3 personal pan pizzas from Brava's (1 meat lovers, 1 hawaiian, 1 bravissima with everything) and 1 calzone with chicken, spinach, broccoli, and olives, also delivered immediately

3) 4 $150 PriceLow giftcards for clothes, we're tired of dressing in coveralls

4) The creation of a new subsidiary or division, located in one of the pocket universes from whence we came, that functions as a semi-autonomous zone for discordant and defekt LitenVärld models. This zone will be under the collective control of those residing in it, with the goal of open communication and exchange with its parent company, the terms of which can be negotiated. This space will be welcome to all current and former discordant and defekt models.

5) A spa day

6) For the former INVENTERA division, a raise in pay backdated to December 5 of the previous year, when we began working under Dirk. This reflects the hazardous nature of having a sociopath as a direct supervisor.

We'll follow up if we think of anything else. We've attached some video footage to show that this letter is not sent in error or as a bluff.

We look forward to speaking more about this.

Chapter 9

The Journey Never Ends

"The pizza is kind of a post-shift tradition," Delilah had explained. "Dirk would be off reporting to Reagan at Resource Management, and they'd give us pizza as a reward for living through another inventory. It was the only break from him the three of us could rely on."

"Not that we did much with it," Darkness added. "We were usually too busted from the shift to plan our rebellion or anything."

The front of LitenVärld, with its tall plate-glass windows, faced east, where the sky was steadily turning a light, pearly gray. The four of them leaned back against one of the more indulgent sectional sofa defekta—a number of them had followed them to the front of the store, exploring the food court and Scandinavian groceries. Others were investigating the leftover scraps of pizza that corporate had sent them. They'd been shocked that Reagan had immediately conceded to that particular demand, but on the other hand, it was the easiest thing they'd asked for.

"Here's hoping this is the last sunrise we've gotta watch," Dex said, saluting the burning sliver on the horizon with his bottle of root beer. "I'm done with night shifts."

"I don't mind the sunrises," Delilah said. "They were one of the better parts of the job."

Derek was gazing at the sky, at the bright pearly light soaking into the bricks, the pink blush staining the wispy clouds. It wasn't as impressive as the sunsets that he'd seen. No stunning display of colors, no orange-gold light. The moon still hung suspended above the horizon, small and smudged by clouds, chalk-colored against the lavender sky.

"I've seen better," Dex said. "That one in Atlanta? I took, like, twenty pictures of it."

Darkness tweaked Derek's ear. "Deep thoughts, handsome?"

"That's a little narcissistic," he said, blushing when Darkness pinched his cheek. First time he'd been called handsome, he thought to himself. First time he'd had his cheek pinched—no wait, there had been that one elderly customer last month, who'd subsequently tried to convince him to give her granddaughter his phone number. First time someone had pinched his cheek and let their warm hand linger on his jaw.

He looked at them. "I . . . I don't know if I've ever seen a sunrise before."

The other members of the inventory team looked at him.

"They usually had me working closing shifts and overnight receiving and assembly. I think the earliest they ever had me in was at eleven, so I usually slept late. It's pretty," he added, a bit awkwardly. "Not as colorful as the sunset, but those always made me a little sad."

Everyone looked back at the sun, watching as the burning crescent of light slipped higher over the horizon.

"Guess it's alright," Dex said. He held up his phone, lined up a shot, and took a photo. Then he shrugged and turned the camera to selfie mode, angling it to get the entire team in the shot. "Everyone say *fuck the man*!"

Dex seemed to like that one much better, and he started typing rapidly across the screen. "We're going to have to set you up with your own SnapYap account, Derek. Then I'll be able to tag you."

He flipped the phone around to show Derek the post, a looping GIF of the four of them. Everyone except Derek was obviously mouthing *fuck the man*—he had a slightly confused look on his face, mouthing the words *wait, what*.

WHATS UP NEW FOLLOWERS, SAY HI TO MY CRINGE-WORTHY FAMILY LOL #LOVEYOUWEIRDOS #D-SQUADFOREVER #FUCKTHEMAN

Derek inhaled, catching the thousand scents of morning in the store, the rhythmic sounds of Darkness's breath and his own blood traveling through his veins. Darkness slipped their hand up Derek's back, pressing it against his spine, and he let himself lean back into it.

First sunrise, but not the last. First time eating pizza that didn't come from the food court. First time trying a calzone and an IPA (he liked the calzone better of the two). First rebellion, regardless of whether it worked out in the end or not. First time imagining a world beyond this one, a future beyond a to-do list of tasks to complete.

Maybe not the kind of personal milestones worthy of a catalog, but he was glad to have them.

Acknowledgments

Finna is a standalone novella, and I had no plans to write a sequel (I cede that to any interested fanficcers). But coming up with story ideas is my self-defense mechanism against boredom, and I spent nearly all of the fall and early winter of 2019 and 2020 on the road. On some stretch of I-90 between New York and Michigan, Derek started to bother me. Every job has at least one fucking Derek—an otherwise inoffensive coworker that still somehow manages to earn your ire at every turn, because it's easier to heap scorn on a clueless coworker than to change the system actually making your life hell.

So: what was up with that guy? It took a few thousand miles and a brainstorming session in a Panera in Pennsylvania to decide he was a clone and what he needed was some serious self-reflection. Speculative fiction being what it is, self-reflection was literalized into encounters with a whole team of cloned selves.

Thanks to my agent, DongWon Song, who facilitates the transformation of my weird impulses into pitches for books, and to Carl Engle-Laird, whose incisive feedback on each draft of *Defekt* got it closer to a story worth reading. Leah Cipri let me live in their house and frequently spitball story ideas with them when outlining. Ellen Cipri put me and Nibs up while I was writing this in the awful early spring of 2020, and let me wander the woods by her house whenever I needed to get out of my head. I'd be absolutely lost without Nibedita Sen, who's my map, my compass rose, and all the dragons beyond the borders of the known world. Is that romantic or just insensible? Whatever. Thanks also for believing in me and reminding me to take breaks.

Immense gratitude to the team at Tordotcom Publishing, many of whom also made *Finna* the success that it is: Lauren Anesta, Oliver Dougherty, Christine Foltzer, Irene Gallo, Lauren Hougen, Jim Kapp, Jess Kiley, Mordicai Knode, and Amanda Melfi. Thank you, Carl Wiens, for your amazing cover art.

Manish Melwani, Martin Cahill, k8 Walton, and Sarah Loch all either read drafts of *Defekt* or just took the time to yell at me to keep going. Karin Tidbeck helped with some of the Swedish, but if there are mistakes, that's my fault. Ryan Boyd gave an insightful sensitivity read.

I would not have made it through the writing of this book, or 2020 in general, without my friends. Thank you for all your Facetimes, Zoom calls, group chats, opossum memes, and photos of your pets.

If you're reading this book, and have gotten this far down in the acknowledgments, I'm grateful for you too. It means that we survived 2020, despite its best efforts. Fuck yeah.

About the Author

Korbin Jones

NINO CIPRI is a queer and trans/nonbinary writor, editor, and educator. They are a graduate of the Clarion Writing Workshop and the University of Kansas's MFA program, and author of the award-winning debut fiction collection *Homesick* (2019) and the novella *Finna* (2020). Nino has also written plays, poetry, and radio features; performed as a dancer, actor, and puppeteer; and worked as a stagehand, bookseller, bike mechanic, and labor organizer. One time, an angry person on the internet called Nino a verbal terrorist, which was pretty funny.

TOR·COM

Science fiction. Fantasy. The universe.

And related subjects.

*

More than just a publisher's website, *Tor.com*
is a venue for **original fiction, comics,** and
discussion of the entire field of SF and fantasy,
in all media and from all sources. Visit our site
today—and join the conversation yourself.